"I highly recommend this Young Adult Historical adventure. It is imaginative enjoyable and enlightening."

Midwest Book Review, Richard R. Blake

"An exciting story you will find difficult to put down."

Between The Lines reviews, Donna Coomer

Other Novels by Charles H. Bertram

CHIPPED BEEF ON TOAST, SOS

STONE BEAR

STONE BEAR And The MAGIC BULLET

RUSTY SON OF TALL ELK

ADVENTURES OF RUSTY

SON OF TALL ELK

by

Charles H. Bertram

INFINITY
PUBLISHING.COM

ISBN 0-7414-5213-8

Published by:

INFINITY
PUBLISHING.COM

1094 New DeHaven Street, Suite 100
West Conshohocken, PA 19428-2713
Info@buybooksontheweb.com
www.buybooksontheweb.com
Toll-free (877) BUY BOOK
Local Phone (610) 941-9999
Fax (610) 941-9959

Printed in the United States of America

Printed on Recycled Paper

Published July 2010

Acknowledgement

Libraries have many reference books about the Native American Indians. Students and writer will find EVERYDAY LIFE among the AMERICAN INDIANS by Candy Moulter most helpful and accurate. ISBN # 0-89879-996-1

Synopsis

Captured and adopted by Cheyenne Indians this red-haired farm boy must use his quick wit and book learning to adjust to his new family. He becomes popular at story telling by adapting white tales to Indian culture. Dressed as a white U.S. marshal, he saves the lives of Cheyenne by tricking some trespassing gold miners to give up without a fight. Rusty is bothered by the killing and torture of them. Keeping secret his ability to read lips becomes a problem. He worries about becoming a renegade to his race as he tries to help his new Cheyenne family defend their way of life.

Characters

Rusty (Russell Weaver)

Tall Elk...Rusty's adopted Cheyenne father

Walking Dove...Rusty's Cheyenne mother, second wife of Tall Elk

Cloud Woman...Tall Elk's first wife

Late Setting Sun...Half-breed daughter of Walking Dove and Hudson Bay trader Quinn, killed when Setting Sun was eight years old

Sam Hiller...Renegade white man that buys and sells guns

White Hawk...Cheyenne warrior

Walks Fast...Most important chief

Burned Face...Cheyenne brave two years older than Rusty, a close friend

Ted Weaver...Rusty's white brother

Gail Weaver...Rusty's white sister

George Weaver...Rusty's older brother

Chapter 1

Montana Territory, Summer 1861

"Rusty, come, bring your rifle! Crow have taken many horses. We can join the war party!" Rusty had seldom seen his friend, Burned Face, move so fast. He was putting his powder horn and bullets in a parfleche, the carryall bag of the plains Indians when his father, Tall Elk, came and took his rifle from its place tied to a lodge pole.

"Can I really go? Shall I bring a second pony?"

"No, that will be your duty. Each brave will have a second horse. You six young braves will follow the party and take care of the tired horses we leave. The Crow will not ride as fast with the horses they took, but they are miles ahead of us. White Hawk will lead. Stay with the other young braves. Hear that my son."

Rusty wears his long red hair in a single braid off to one side. In it he wears two eagle feathers. He is now much tanner and most of the freckles he had when first captured are gone.

The five young braves and Rusty rode in the dust of the war party that was in pursuit of the horse stealing Crow. Red Falcon, son of Twisted Nose, was in charge. All were armed and hoping they would get a chance to fight or count coup. Rusty was the best armed with the new Hawkins rifle and a Colt six-shot pistol. Burned Face had his short stagecoach shotgun that he was proud of. He had decorated the stock with brass tacks. He rode a roan pony with two handprints painted on it, one for the gold miner and one for the Crow he had killed. Rusty's pony had six painted hands, one of which had a line across it, meaning that it was a shared kill. His sister, Late Setting Sun, made that mark for the Crow she had hit with her fish spear, saving Rusty's life.

They pushed their ponies, following the dust of the warriors across the rolling plains east of the Rocky Mountains and north of the Yellow Stone River, the land claimed by the Northern Cheyenne, a claim confirmed by the treaty of 1825 that allowed wagons going to Oregon on the Bozeman trail to cut through their land.

"There, look! We have a rider following us," said Likes To Sing.

"It must be your sister, Setting Sun. She is becoming a manly-woman," said Burned Face.

"I never heard a person called that. What does it mean?"

It means, Rusty, my friend, that she is still a woman, but can do many things as good as a man. Things like race and fight."

"Then, am I to blame for teaching her?"

"No, Rusty, long before you came, she was beginning to be strong and would challenge boys in races. Here she comes. Are you going to order her back to the village?"

"She will not listen to me, but I will try."

"Does the family know you are joining us, my sister? I don't think your father, Tall Elk, would like you being here. It is my place to order you to return to your girl duties."

"Two of the horses taken were mine. Why are you braves riding so slow?"

"Our fighting braves are each using two ponies. When one is runout, he will change mounts. This will make them ride faster than the Crow. We are to take care of the mounts that the warriors turn loose. It will get to be hard when they have left us some tired horses and we must keep following them and not let the ponies get so far behind. We must count them and when we have all, return them to the tribe's herd. You ride with Rusty at your side," said Red Falcon.

"Is your rifle loaded?"

"No, I came too quick, I can load it while riding."

"Do so, sister warrior; it is just a heavy stick without powder and ball," said Rusty.

In two hours they began to find ponies walking or standing and grazing the rich grass. An hour later, with most of the ponies now in their charge, they began to have a string over a half mile long.

Several miles ahead of them, a brave rode to White Hawk, the leader of this pursuit.

"There are not as many tracks of horses with riders. Some have used the low hills to cover their leaving. Do you think they are going back to our main herd?"

"How many?" said White Hawk.

"Maybe five..., six, not ten. Shall we send word to the village?"

"No, they know we have dropped off horses and may only have a few young braves to take them. I will send some fighting braves back to protect our horses and young braves." He rode to Tall Elk and told him about the missing Crow.

"Send four braves back."

"No, Tall Elk, two will do. The Crow have few rifles, many of our young braves have guns. But send them now, two good fighters."

Running Bear and Blue Scar, two veteran warriors, were not pleased about going back but obeyed their leaders.

With the addition of Setting Sun, there were seven young braves. Two were now in the very rear. The rest were on both sides of the front, herding the loose horses. Rusty had grown tired of Setting Sun's complaining. He was riding too close and had traded sides with Gray Wolf. When the six Crow attacked, they came riding hard with war whoops, screaming, and war clubs held high, three to each side. Rusty used his Hawkins rifle and dropped one before they got within arrow range. Burned Face held his short shotgun down low and out of sight till the last minute. His first blast nearly took off the head of a Crow Indian. He missed with his second shot as the next Crow ducked, and rode at Rusty, then he was shot by Rusty's pistol. Red Falcon rode to the other side. Setting Sun got off her pony, rested her rifle over it, and shot one Crow brave. Red Falcon, Gray Wolf, and Likes To Sing attacked the two with rifles and war clubs. Both Crow ran. One had the bad luck to run into Running Bear who speared him with a lance. Running Bear looked around and called to Red Falcon.

"You know what to do. Keep these ponies here in a tight group. Your young braves made a good fight. We will go."

The young braves and Setting Sun just sat at first, the combat had happened so fast.

"Load all guns!" called Rusty.

"Yes, be ready if more Crow are willing for us to kill them," said Red Falcon as he took charge. "You two, round up the Crow horses. Stay together. Let us put all the Crow war clubs and bows in a pile, here," he pointed by the dead Crow that Burned Face had shot.

Rusty was shocked when Setting Sun scalped the Crow she killed. The others also scalped and counted coup. No one questioned that he didn't scalp his kills. Rusty did not count coup on the dead with his hand. By now they knew it was not his way to scalp and they respected his not doing so.

"Burned Face, that gun of yours is like an army cannon. Will you trade it?"

"No, my good friend, son of Twisted Nose, but you should know it is not like a rifle, it is no good but up close.

Even a bow and arrow can kill at greater range. It spreads the little balls till only a few will hit beyond as far as you can throw a tomahawk. But yes, up close, the shotgun is powerful, and hard to miss with, but I just did."

The waiting was hard on the young braves after the excitement of the fight.

Gray Wolf was trying to draw Setting Sun into talking with him when he said, "Setting Sun, is your brother still helping you to read? Read the white man's words so you can be a reader of stories like he is?"

Rusty did not want to answer and hurt her feelings, since his efforts to teach her were a failure. The reading book he had for beginners was from England and when he read from it to show her what the words were, she threw the book into the fire, saying, "This is no good, you don't talk that way!" Their tempers and stubbornness clashed till both agreed he was done teaching her. Setting Sun shot a rabbit and began to make a cooking fire.

"Do you have some magic that you can feed all of us with one rabbit?" asked Red Falcon.

"Yes, in the village it is a squaw's duty to feed the men; but you are not men, we are not in the village and I know all of you can shoot rabbits. This meat is for the family of Tall Elk." She skinned and cleaned the rabbit and put it on a lance from the dead Crow. Her fire was of buffalo chips and the smell of cooking meat soon had the young braves out hunting, until Red Falcon ruled that only two could go at a time and then to stay close. Only one more rabbit was found. When its meat was shared, Rusty cut up theirs and all had at least a leg.

"Look, see the dust? A herd," cried Gray Wolf. White Hawk led the party back, one brave was wounded and riding double to keep him from falling off. Rusty counted and found that two more were missing. They seemed to be returning with more horses that were taken by the Crow. The young braves were too eager to return to the village and Tall Elk made Rusty and Burned Face stay and do a better job of putting out the cooking fires.

For the rest of the day, the village was a place of mourning and wailing. The wounded brave had also died. Rusty learned that, in addition to the five Crow killed by them and Running Bear, ten or more had fallen to the Cheyenne rifles and arrows. The Crow had foolishly sent many of their braves to protect the returning horse raiding party and they got to the fight too late. The Cheyenne had caught up, and using their advantage of weapons, had killed or run off the horse-stealing Crow. They had time to reload their rifles when the village Crows reached them. A five-to-one advantage in rifles sent the Crow running to protect their village.

Running Bear and White Hawk led a horse-stealing raid of their own and gathered up twenty of the Crow horses. The success of the day took two nights of speeches, telling and re-telling about the battles. Rusty, thanks in part to his reading to the groups, had become a skillful speaker and was able to act out what happened with exaggeration. He used gestures of Burned Face being almost knocked off his horse by the recoil of his shotgun and pulling a blanket up, played the Crow having his head shot off. He did Setting Sun not just scalping, but using her teeth to pull off the scalp, dancing around with it, and cutting out the heart and roasting it like the rabbit. His act had to be repeated several times.

Then Setting Sun warned him to make fun of her no more or else. He knew what the "or else" meant and skipped over her part, except for her shooting over the back of a pony. Twisted Nose spoke, praising Red Falcon for his leadership and his niece Setting Sun and nephew Rusty for their bravery. Tall Elk stood holding two of the Hawkins rifles that Sam Hiller, the renegade gun dealer, had sold them. He held his and Rusty's high for all to see.

"Rusty, my son, tell the people about the wood of these rifles."

This came as a surprise to the boy, as he was sure Tall Elk would know it meant he would have to tell some about his life with his white family, a telling he was advised to avoid. He took his rifle and held it high.

"The wood on this fine rifle has a twisting pattern. It is known as curly maple, it is rare and it's from the maple tree that has hard wood, not the soft one that gives the sap that is sweet. I was with my brothers and uncle taking some logs, trees of this curly maple, to the white man's city of St. Louis, where the two big rivers meet. We had two long rafts of logs. I was on shore to make an evening fire for cooking when white men river pirates took my boat and left me to be found by White Hawk and my uncle, Twisted Nose." Tall Elk held up a hand for Rusty to wait.

"There are here tonight some Cheyenne that joined we, of the Raven clan, in the last few moons. They should know that my son, Rusty, has to thank the spirits for his red hair. My brother, Twisted Nose, was east of the big river with our friend, Sam Hiller, the gun buyer, when they found this son of mine. Twisted Nose saw that red hair as White Hawk was about to cut the white boy's throat. He knew that I and Walking Dove had Late Setting Sun of the same age, also with hair the color of fire. That is the reason this son of mine is here to speak." He sat and indicated for Rusty to go on.

"The wood, curly maple, is extra hard and the trees from where I lived as a small white boy were sold to the Hawkins gun makers in St. Louis. This rifle with the rare wood stock has strong medicine for me, because I knew the tree that was used to make the stock for my rifle. That medicine was there when I shot the first of the four Crows we young braves killed." He looked and saw that Tall Elk was pleased. So he sat and his rifle was passed around and the wood was looked at by the light of the council fire. As he sat, Rusty watched the elders speaking, even those too far from him to hear. He practiced his lip reading, a skill none but the gun dealer, Sam Hiller, knew about. He was soon sorry he had read the lips of Chief Walks Fast and his squaw, Berry Woman. She asked if he had seen the boy blush when his sister Setting Sun warned him to make fun of her no more.

"Yes, I saw. His sister had always been able to make his face turn red, ever since she spanked him."

* * * * * *

The ten-year-old Rusty arrived at the Cheyenne village as a captive. He was tired and sore from four days of hard riding. Russell Richard Weaver was a freckled, red haired, skinny farm boy with dimples and a constant smile. His nickname was Rusty. His sister-to-be was Late Setting Sun, a half-Irish, half-Cheyenne girl with red hair, deep black almond shaped eyes and skin much more fair than the other Indian girls. She was also the most attractive. She was one year older and one inch taller than he. She was given what was to the Cheyenne a routine chore. She was to see that he changed into the dress of the Cheyenne. His shyness and stubbornness conflicted with her temper and obligation to duty. "I'm not taking off my pants in front of a strange girl!" Pants without underwear at that. "You don't know how to wear these leggings and breechcloth!" The girl tripped him and, sitting on his back, removed his pants to discover a very white rear end that had bright red freckles, which made her laugh. She spanked him to force his cooperation for the dressing, a spanking, that with the freckled rear, she would tease him about for a long time.

* * * * * *

When Rusty was nine years old, he was sick with childhood illnesses that had him in bed for several weeks. A lady was hired as a nurse to sit and read with him. This lady was the daughter of the owner of a gunpowder factory in Alton, Illinois. There had been an explosion and she was caught in the open delivering pay slips. The blast made her deaf. Her wealthy father sent her to Boston, where at the Boston School For The Deaf, she learned to read lips. Alexander Graham Bell was one of her teachers. That skill she taught to Rusty, with a warning that it can cause trouble when you know what people say and they don't know that you know. He had found that to be true and had made trouble one time for his new sister, Setting Sun.

* * * * * *

Scouts began to report that white gold miners were again moving into the land of the Cheyenne. There had been a visit from some blue coat soldiers who told the Cheyenne they were not to kill those miners but ask them to leave and tell them that the army would come and make them leave. This the Cheyenne laughed at. The head chief, Walks Fast, and several braves including White Hawk, the war chief, left to see these miners for themselves. While they were gone, three men from a wagon train came to speak. One of the white men was an older mountain man they knew. With him was a trader who claimed to be a friend of Sam Hiller and a white man dressed as a Cherokee Indian. Tall Elk met them and gave them food and a pipe to smoke before talking about what they wanted. Rusty was allowed to come out of hiding when the mountain man asked for him and told Tall Elk he had words for the boy and his father and not to fear his sending soldiers to take him away.

"What is the reason for this visit?" asked Tall Elk.

The mountain man who was wearing a well-worn buckskin jacket and leggings spoke. "The Cheyenne have been my friends for a long time. I, Jim Bridger, spent one winter with your Shaman, Red Hatchet, at a village above the Yellow Stone River. This man," he pointed to the white man dressed as a Cherokee, "is the famous tracker, 'The White Cherokee.' He is here to trade with you. You have my word he is to be trusted." Then he sat.

A tall older man dressed in fine deerskin and a mix of white man's pants and Cherokee marked garments rose to speak. But his knowledge of Cheyenne was so poor that Tall Elk asked him to speak in English. He and his son, Rusty, Dreams A Lot, would translate.

"I have lived with the Cherokee for many years. My Cherokee people now live on reservations and in the south. I have been hired to meet with the Cheyenne about some wagons that are soon passing through the lands of the Cheyenne. The people of this group of wagons are good people; they know that the horses, cattle and mules will eat some of the grass as they pass. Some will want to shoot game for fresh meat. I know the proud Cheyenne would not sell what the great spirit has given them in game and grass. But these people, being good, wish to give gifts to the Cheyenne in return for the gifts of that grass and game. I will see that no white men shoot recklessly and only wish that the Cheyenne, unlike the Crow," here he spat on the ground, "will not try and steal their horses and mules."

Tall Elk spoke himself. "Show us these gifts."

The trader opened one of three packs and spread a blanket. Then he put on it bags of coffee, sugar and many twists of tobacco. He saw no look of joy on the face of Tall Elk, so after a nod from the White Cherokee, he opened a second pack and took out bags of beads, some rolls of red cloth, knives and trinkets. Tall Elk spoke. "The men on the last wagons had many cattle and yet they shot at deer and buffalo and there was a danger of them spreading the white man's sickness into the water used by the Cheyenne. These are poor gifts for so much trouble. Take your gifts and go around our land."

The White Cherokee opened the last pack and made two piles, one of one-pound tins of gunpowder and one of bars of lead.

"The winters here are long. The Cheyenne will need to shoot many buffalo for meat; this will help them." He pointed to the last two piles.

"I will talk with some of the elders," said Tall Elk as he walked away after indicating the white men should stay.

Rusty saw the opportunity to speak and addressed the one called White Cherokee.

"I was a white boy before, now I am a Cheyenne brave. You are white. Why are you a Cherokee? Were you captured as a boy?"

"No, I came to this land from across the waters. The English were going to hang me as a poacher. The Cherokee welcomed me." Rusty then had the job of explaining what a poacher was.

"He was a trapper of game from the lands of...of a chief that wanted all game for himself."

Rusty looked at a smiling White Cherokee, who said, "I took game like you steal horses."

Rusty repeated that and it was understood. The mountain man asked Rusty to step away from the group.

"Boy, you should know that a powerful enemy is after your red scalp. Black Knife of the Crow says you killed his son. He tells all that one day he will come for you and not to kill, but to take you back for torture. He feels only that will give his son peace in the happy hunting ground. He is ashamed his warrior son was killed by a young white boy. Be careful! He's as mean and clever as they make 'em."

The White Cherokee heard this and said he would also speak with Rusty.

"I had a son that would be your age now. He was killed by buffalo hunters. My daughter died on The Trail-Of-Tears. You seem to have made a life for yourself here. Good, but in coming years, your Cheyenne may, like my Cherokee, suffer from the whites' greed for gold and land. You should always be prepared to fight or flee. Sometimes a man has no choice. My advice is to take advantage of your white skin. You should have a shirt and pants with boots and jacket and a hat, against the day it may be safer for you to dress as a white man to avoid being shot by the army. There is a big war now between the north and south. That is why there are so few soldiers in the west. That war will not last, they are killing so many it is hard to believe. When it is over, there will be many soldiers still wanting to prove what great leaders they are. The Indians will be their enemy. What treaties say is worthless," here he spit. "So good luck, young brave."

Tall Elk returned and agreed to take the gifts and gave his word this wagon train would pass the lands of the Cheyenne with no fear, as long as the whites with the wagons did not break the words that this White Cherokee had promised.

Chapter 2

"Rusty, come with me. Yes, take your rifle. No, Setting Sun, stay here," said Tall Elk.

"Where are we going?" asked Rusty.

"Not something that I think we should be doing. You are to take the place of Sam Hiller and speak to miners in their fort. You will have to wear white man's clothes and speak with a man's voice. White Hawk will tell you more. But listen to me and be careful you don't get shot. Come this way."

They rode for four hours, stopping only to rest the horses. Rusty could see they were riding towards the stream where gold miners had been found before. At the edge of woods, they were met by a brave who told them to wait there. White Hawk soon rode up and handed Rusty a bundle. He spoke to Tall Elk but made sure Rusty understood his words.

"There are eight miners left. We killed four. They have built a fort. It would cost many braves to kill them. They have long shooting buffalo guns and food and water. I sent for Sam Hiller, the gun seller, but he is far away. I wish Rusty to dress in these and tell the whites that he is from the army and they must leave. He is to say, "If they will go without a fight, the Cheyenne will let them ride out and keep their scalps.""

The bundle was the clothes of a white man. There was a bullet hole and blood stains.

"Can you do this, my son?" asked Tall Elk.

"Yes, Father and White Hawk, I want to. It may save the lives of our braves. I will know what words to say. I should have a tall horse and maybe a blanket to sit on to look older."

"He will speak from deep in the trees. I don't want him shot!" said Tall Elk.

"White Hawk, when I yell, 'Cease fire,' it means no shooting. You must tell all braves 'NO SHOOTING' when I say those words. They will obey you." Rusty changed clothes and rode closer to the stream. The Cheyenne were all around the miners' small fort, hiding behind trees, a fort on the streambed made of logs and dirt piles. The trees gave them protection from the rifles of the miners.

Rusty practiced making his voice as deep as he could, then rode as close as he dared.

"Hold your fire! Hello in the stream, hold your fire! This is U.S. Marshal Weaver, fourth district. Don't shoot, I am unarmed and coming closer."

Rusty stopped while he was still partly hidden by brush and as close as Tall Elk would allow.

A miner called out. "Marshal, do you have troops with you?"

"I have my two deputies, both Cheyenne. The Cheyenne here from Walks Fast tribe will listen to me. You should never have come here. The treaty has set this land for the Cheyenne. I can get you out alive, that is all I promise. There are a hundred braves here, most with rifles. If you turn yourselves over to me, I will guarantee your safe passage to the fort, or the trail where there are many wagons. But you must put down your guns. You may only take what you can carry. All mining equipment to be left here. Your horses are already gone. I can only hold these Cheyenne back for a short time. Now, walk out, without guns, or I will have no choice but to pull out myself and hope I can get back alive when they rush you and the shooting starts. Well, what is it to be?"

"Marshal, how come you don't come closer?"

"Because I don't trust your trigger happy men."

The miners argued for a spell and yelled, "You sure you can guarantee we walk out with our scalps if we give up?"

"Put down your guns and I'll ride out to supervise your safe passage. Walks Fast band will not shoot me."

Rusty pulled away the rope that Tall Elk was holding on Rusty's horse.

Four miners walked out of the improvised log fort and stacked some rifles. Rusty rode closer. He turned and spoke to braves that were not there so they could not see his face. His braids were hidden by a large hat. He was calling, "Hold your fire, no shooting." When all seven miners came out, some grumbling, he called, "Where is your other man? Does he hold a gun on me?"

"No, he's hit in the leg. Here is his rifle." Rusty counted eight rifles and three pistols. While the miners were gathering food supplies, Rusty saw White Hawk signal braves to move in.

Just as the spokesman for the miners called, "Where the hell are your deputies?", White Hawk screamed in Cheyenne, "Open fire! Shoot! Kill all!"

The miners to a man fell under a hail of bullets. Smoke from the black powder filled the streambed. Rusty felt betrayed. The screams of the wounded man from inside the fort were also upsetting to him. He was sure the man was being scalped while alive. And maybe getting more torture than he wanted to know about.

"Good words! You saved many squaws from weeping tonight," said a pleased White Hawk. Walks Fast came over and told Tall Elk he could be proud of his son. Rusty looked at the twisted bodies now being scalped and ran to throw up in the woods. He recalled what the White Cherokee had said, and saved the clothes, and added a pair of boots and a coat. "We might need to do this again," he said as he tied the bundle to his saddlebag, once back in the dress of a Cheyenne. Walks Fast told Tall Elk that his son looked pale. "Have a brave escort him back to the village. The miners and all traces of their being here will be removed. I want it done so none will know they dug for gold here. I put you, Tall Elk, in charge of doing that as I know you will see it is done."

Tall Elk had the braves gather all the belongings of the miners. He took an ax and broke the four whiskey jugs, to the dismay of some of them helping him. He allowed them to take what they could use. The only food that was not taken was some old bacon. Since he was the leader, he only took a bag of coffee beans and a bag of sugar, and those after no one else wanted one of the two coffee pots. All the iron cooking gear was loaded onto the miners' horses to give to those in the village that would want them.

"All the rifles and pistols will be given to the braves that did this fighting, but the council will say who is to have what gun. Those without a good rifle will have the first choice," said Tall Elk as he gave braves duties of burying what was not taken. Even the horse droppings of the miners' horses were cleaned up. Rusty watched that being done till he left with a brave who was pleased to leave the cleaning up of horse droppings and ride with Rusty back to the village.

At the council fire that night, Rusty was praised. White Hawk asked Tall Elk to have his son stand. He was holding a rolled up blanket. With a speech that was too long for Rusty, he gave Rusty the blanket and motioned for him to open it. Inside was a rifle like none he had ever seen. It was like a cross of a Colt revolver and a rifle. Rusty read the writing on the barrel. Colt model 1855, .44 caliber military carbine model. It was a new rifle that fired six shots. The barrel was only twenty inches long since it was a carbine. It came from the miners. With it came a brass powder measurer and a bullet mold.

"This gun that fires many shots, and is powerful, will protect our Cheyenne son, Dreams A Lot...Rusty, son of Tall Elk," said White Hawk.

Rusty didn't need lip reading to hear White Hawk tell Chief Walks Fast, "These were poor miners. We found they had not taken much gold for all the gravel they moved. We had many braves helping us hide where the stream was dug into for gold."

Rusty was still upset and went to the lodge early. Setting Sun joined him.

"Hello, Marshal Weaver! You should be pleased, yet you look sad. I don't understand," she said.

"Every time I get to thinking I want only to be a Cheyenne, something like this happens. I was made to be a liar, a Judas goat. I tricked the miners and they were slaughtered. It was not right."

"You think too much like a God man. Should we let the miners come and take our land? Should our braves die to protect our lodges? Would not the whites do the same to save lives? I am proud to have you as a brother."

"Your words are true, sister, yet I feel bad. What will I do in the morning if I feel this way? I welcome your advice."

She picked up the Colt rifle. "We go and test this gun that shoots six times like a pistol but is a true rifle. May I shoot with you?"

"I would gladly give this gun to you; it will always make me feel bad, but that would not bring honor to White Hawk or our father, so I must keep it. If it works as well as I think, I shall give you my pistol. I don't need two that shoot six shots."

The next morning, Rusty waited till Setting Sun was free to join him. He set up a target at the base of one side of the stream banks where the bullets could do no harm and where he could recover the lead for re-casting. His first shot was a surprise. "This gun just bit me!" he looked at his forearm. There were powder burns on his wrist. He showed it to Setting Sun. "Where the bullets go from the cylinder to the barrel there is a gap, and some of the fire jumps out." He scratched his arm. "Even a little shaving of lead!" For the next shot, he held the rifle with both hands behind the cylinder. This grip didn't give him as steady of a hold as his rifle, but it shot far better than the pistol.

Setting Sun put her hand on his wrist. "If you had a piece of hide you could slip on, that would protect your arm and you could put one hand on the barrel." *I will have Cloud Woman make it of hard, thick hide,* she thought.

"Yes, but the barrel is already getting hot. I'll try and add a wood front stock, one that I can hold and will not stick up in the way of the sights."

"Look, it loads like a pistol. There is no need to use a long ramrod. This small rod under the barrel sets the bullets in the cylinder."

"Here, you try shooting it." He was done reloading and gave it to her.

"It's heavier than it looks." She took aim, holding both hands behind the cylinder. With each shot she came closer till the last two were dead center.

"We should back up and see how well it shoots at rifle range. This is only a little more than pistol range." Rusty loaded while she paced off steps till she was sure it was not real long, but rifle range.

Rusty took a stick and drew a deer in the mud of the stream bank, with the skin target now as the heart. Each took three shots and walked back to the target. Two hits were in the heart, three were close, and one was off target. Setting

Sun used a stick and checked three hits, one in the heart, and two others not far off. Rusty did not say a thing when she pointed to the miss and to him. He did that on purpose when he saw his first hit was true.

"This gun is hot, and so am I," he said, and they walked back to the lodge. Setting Sun took it and carried the rifle when they passed some boys. Rusty pulled out his pistol and gave it to his sister. Setting Sun thanked him with a hug and kiss on a cheek. He blushed and the women laughed.

"Rusty will be an old man and still blush," said Setting Sun.

"No, not an old brave, but it is true that Setting Sun is best at making her brother's face turn the color of his hair," said Walking Dove, with a wink to Setting Sun. Rusty gave Setting Sun a fake smile and left.

Rusty went for a walk. He was having trouble getting over his role in deceiving the miners. His mood was not helped by the reference to Sun's ability to make him blush.

At times like this, he could not help going back to that first day as a Cheyenne. He had been so tired. He was tied on so he would not fall off his horse. Four hard days of riding. Then this girl, now his sister, was given the chore of getting him into the dress of a brave. He had refused to take off his pants in front of a strange girl, or any girl for that matter. She had tripped him, ripped off his pants, and then spanked his rear till he gave in and let her dress him with a breechcloth and leggings. For a year she had teased him about the spanking and his white rear end with freckles. He had thought her promise to stop was good, till she said "or else" at the council fire. That spanking by a girl was like a bad visitor, always returning whenever he got into a bad mood. This walk was not helping him with his mood.

He was considering going on a second vision quest. The weather was mild. Then his name was called.

"Rusty, Iron Hand would like to see you. Can you come now?" It was Long Bow, the short brave who worked with the maker of arrowheads, spear points, and general fixer of weapons. Long Bow's name was a joke, since he was very short, and, as a boy, used a bow that was bigger than he was. He would hold it sideways to shoot arrows. He was highly skilled at working with flint and since Rusty had begun sharing with his master, Iron Hand, what Rusty had observed at the Blacksmith in Silver Creek, Illinois. He now worked with iron and steel more than flint.

"These old bones have not seen you for some time. I take pride in the knives we are making since you got me better tools." Rusty noted that he did not say, "Since you taught me to temper iron and steel when the color of the metal was cherry red." "You did a great service to our people when you tricked the fool miners into putting down their guns." He had Long Bow bring out some more scraps of iron and steel. The wagon trains that passed through their lands were breaking down or having to reduce loads. This source of steel and iron was first discovered by Rusty, and now the dog soldiers and hunters were bringing things to Iron Hand. Long Bow opened the flap on the small lodge where Iron Hand worked.

"Now, Rusty, Dreams A Lot, what can I do for the clever young son of Tall Elk that saved so many lives at the stream?"

"I...Long Bow said you wanted to see me?" said Rusty.

"Look here!" He took a blanket off a pile of metal. He held up a pike bayonet and spoke. "This was what we used to make that short spear. Do you wish to have a second? I will make it for you, with help from Long Bow, as a gift from Chief Walks Fast." The short spear was the javelin that Rusty carried.

So that was what this was all about, thought Rusty. The chief thanking him for his role in deceiving the gold miners that were all killed. He remembered that he should hold Iron Hand in respect. Rusty pointed to the pike bayonet.

"I wish to take that and make a knife like this." He drew a dagger, a long thin one, in the dirt.

"This is a knife to kill with, for sticking, not cutting. You wish that?" questioned Iron Hand.

"It is called by the white men an Arkansas toothpick. A great defensive weapon. I wish it as a gift for my mother, or maybe sister."

"And what can I make for you?" he said.

Rusty saw a broken file. "Here is great metal for a special knife." He drew a Bowie knife. "I would want to work with you in making it."

"Yes, what does this word Bowie mean?" asked the old man as he tapped the file with a hammer and smiled at the sound of very hard steel.

"Jim Bowie was a great warrior. His name by the Creek Indians was, 'Knife-that-cuts-two ways.' See, the top third of the blade is as sharp as the whole lower edge. Bowie was killed by the Mexicans at a place called the Alamo."

"I will have Long Bow make much charcoal and send for you when it is ready. Thank you for coming."

Rusty left, looking back to see Long Bow heading for the big lodge of Chief Walks Fast. *He's going to report, good,* thought Rusty, now not in such a bad mood.

Rusty returned to the lodge to again find a line of young bucks waiting and hoping to see Setting Sun. She had recently had her second menstrual period and was much coveted as a wife. Young bucks would ask Rusty to put in a good word for them with her. She made no bones about not being interested at this time in being the squaw for anyone. Rusty would joke with her about the bucks. He would start off with a name who had asked him to speak for him, then add names till he was up to a dozen or more, making up some of them or using the names of older men from the group called Fat Bellies who no longer hunted. This time he added the name of his best friend, Burned Face, to see her reaction.

"You should not joke about him. He is our best friend. Do you know how he got burned? I think not because you were told not to ask. I shall tell you. Because I have a reason and know two somethings you don't about him. Sixteen summers ago there was a wagon with sick white people that stopped for water. The same day a hunting party of Cheyenne braves also stopped there for water. Later, the whole of their village became sick, many died. Their lodges were set on fire. A squaw heard a papoose cry from a lodge that was on fire. She pushed in the poles and pulled out a blanket that was on fire and had a boy child that was being burned. She dumped some soup that was there on him and only half of his face was burned. All his people were dead, and no one wanted him. His chief gave him to an older brave and his woman that had lost their young to the sickness. They died when he was eleven or so summers old, and he was allowed to live on his own in their teepee. Tall Elk and Chief Walks Fast have always looked out for him as a lucky child. That is one thing. Do you want to hear the second?"

"Yes, and thanks for telling me that. I always wondered about the burn scars on his face. So what is there to tell?"

"He is to have a woman of his own! And soon."

"How can that be? I don't know about this. No one has said anything! I even talked to him this morning."

"His bride to be is not of our tribe. The village she is from had some sickness. White Weasel, the medicine man, is having her wait alone in the young girls' hut for five days to be sure she brings no sickness. She came two days ago while you were gone tricking the miners."

"What is she? What tribe? What is she like? How did this happen?"

"One question at a time, little brother. Her name is Pigeon Girl. She is Sioux. She was found and brought here by our hunters; they found her on the prairie. She had a bad cut on the side of her nose. They say her father believed she was too friendly with too many bucks. She said that was not so. He was beginning to cut off her nose. She hit his hand and ran off, taking his fastest horse. The horse broke a leg in a prairie dog hole, and she walked away. They let her go. Chief Walks Fast knew that Burned Face was ready to have a squaw. You should have been there. Walks Fast asked Burned Face if he wanted her, with her there. He said yes but only if she wanted him. She asked him if he would beat her or cut her nose off. He said only if she gave him the need to do so. She asked if he wanted children, he said yes. She took a blanket and put it on the ground and sat, waiting to be carried to his lodge on a blanket as a sign of their bring married. Walks Fast let them carry her, but then listened to White Weasel, and the medicine man took her to where she now waits. Let's ask Tall Elk if we can have a feast for Burned Face."

"Yes, a feast," said Tall Elk. Our lodge has always looked on Burned Face as a kind of son. I will send hunters for some elk or deer. Setting Sun, you will help with the cooking, and Rusty...he has been your friend, you must be the crier and sing words of praise of Burned Face. And to please the people you should tell one of your funny stories."

From the beginning when Rusty had been asked to read newspapers then books, he had gained a following as a speaker and storyteller. It started when he had to make up stories because what was in the few books were both words hard to read and explain. He made up tales, then learned to exaggerate and add the acting out of parts. He learned that storytelling was a popular recreation during evening and winters. One time when the only book he had was one he was tired of, he pretended to be reading while he recited The Charge of the Light Brigade by Alfred Lord Tennyson. He had memorized it for a fourth of July celebration. Now what to come up with for his best friend? He walked around trying to think of something, all the events of his and Burned Face the last three years had been done several times. He wanted something different, a new story.

Rusty spent most of the next two days working with Iron Hand on the knives. The first Bowie knife was bigger than Rusty meant it to be. When hammered out, the file made a good Bowie knife but a foot long. They used a broken part of a two-handed lumber saw to make a second Bowie knife only nine inches long. Rusty liked that one and said he would give the bigger one as a wedding gift. The Arkansas toothpick he would give to Setting Sun. He was taking it back to their lodge and met Setting Sun.

"What do you have, baby brother?"

He had not planned what to say when giving the knife to her, and now she started that "baby brother" stuff again, he knew she had reached fourteen summers and he now was only twelve for another month. Then he would be only a year younger by his figuring.

"Here, I made this for you to stick your enemies with, like you stick me about the first day we met." They talked while walking towards the lodge.

"Oh! You mean the time I spanked your freckled butt? I had forgotten all about that years ago."

"Liar! This knife is called an Arkansas toothpick. It's a well-known style in the deep south. Good protection for little girls."

Setting Sun pulled his arm. "Wait, if you really made this for me, it is a fine and important gift, I thank you." Then she hugged and quickly kissed him, not on his cheek, but on the mouth, and ran into their lodge.

Did she kiss me because of the gift, or to get at the three young bucks that were watching, waiting to see if she would speak to one of them, Rusty thought.

Chapter 3

The feast for Burned Face and Pigeon Girl was the next night. Rusty found some paper and made a list of the good things he could say about his friend. He still had not planned on what he could say as entertainment. He started to go for a ride and saw the two braves guarding the horses speak. He read the lips of one. He said, "If Rusty, son of Tall Elk, goes for a ride, he gets talking to himself and waving his arms up and down."

"Did Setting Sun's kiss do that?" said one of them. "You can stay here. I'm going to look for Voice Like A Man, she is more fun. Even if when standing under a blanket she only talks."

That evening there was first dancing, then eating, more dancing and at last the speeches. Some told about what a fine brave Burned Face was, and how lucky was this Sioux girl to have him as her man. Tall Elk even spoke about the fine role Burned Face did in helping his son, Dreams A Lot, learn the ways of the Cheyenne. By the time it was Rusty's turn, he felt that there was little left to say. But as custom required, he repeated much of the praise about his friend. Then he walked near to the council fire for all to see and hear, and stood.

"I, Dreams A Lot...Rusty, son of Tall Elk, will speak!"

26

He waved his arms in an animated manner making the sign language of clouds and a head filled with dreams. Signs that what he was to say was not true.

"First you should know that in other parts of this great world men are tried by fire. They proved themselves as men by walking with bare feet on fire.

"I will tell you friends of Burned Face a story.... 'Once upon a time...,' he was sure they all would remember these as the lines from the fairy tales he had told..., 'there was far on the other side of the big river a small boy lost in the woods. He came upon two great Cheyenne warriors and a friend of theirs, a white man gun peddler.'" He saw people look at each other and wonder. Many looked at Tall Elk and Walking Dove, who made signs that they had no idea of what he was about to tell. "That boy had green hair and funny skin. He was at the wrong place at the wrong time. He tried to hide under a juniper tree from the fierce Cheyenne. He did not know, since he was but a little white boy, that his tracks told where he was hiding. He was pulled out and a knife was put to his throat. 'Stop! Don't cut him. This boy has GREEN HAIR!'" While speaking, Rusty was acting with exaggerated motions. As a small boy, he bent to be shorter, and even stuck his thumb in his mouth. "The fierce Cheyenne with the knife said, 'I want this green hair on my lance.' 'No!' said the other. 'There is a chief, Little Fawn, he has a daughter with green hair. The poor girl is homely, and has no friends, she is shy, it would be good to take this boy to join her.'

"So this poor little white boy was put on a horse and he rode for a long time, riding fast to stay ahead of Crow, Arapaho and Apache. By the time they reached the Cheyenne village, his bottom was like an over pounded pemmican. It was as sore as a snake bite. He had no sleep for ten days and was given to the girl with green hair. She was to help him change from white man's clothes to the dress of the Cheyenne. But he was shy, and would not take off his pants.

Unlike the Cheyenne, he was not proud of the body the great spirit gave him. He fought the girl to keep his clothes. The fight was so great that their throwing each other on the ground made the pony herd think there was a buffalo stampede. He was losing the fight because he was so tired from lack of sleep.

"The girl with green hair fought like a girl, biting and scratching, until to this day his skin still has little red marks. Marks some would say are freckles. She won and got him dressed. Only winning because she hit him on his sore bottom! And this poor little white boy, by this trial of fire, FIRE on his butt, became a true Cheyenne." He now walked tall and with his chest out as he said "true Cheyenne." "You all know that this is just a story and could never have happened!"

Everyone enjoyed the story so much that at times he had to repeat what he said because the laughing made it hard to hear. All were still talking about it when Setting Sun stood and waved her arms to speak.

"Burned Face has been my friend, so I must help my brother, that poor little lost white boy, get his story right.... Once upon a time, two Cheyenne braves found a poor, wet, lost white boy with freckles and BLUE hair. 'No! Don't scalp him. There is a village where they like children with hair of many colors.' But a great Cheyenne warrior put his knife to the boy's throat and scared the boy so much his hair turned from blue to white. White as snow or the hair of a very old brave. The boy shook from fear and when they tied him to a horse, the rope went under his arm and he giggled, for he was very ticklish because his face was cute like a baby's. He was taken to their village. There, a beautiful daughter of an important chief was chosen to help him dress correctly as a Cheyenne. He fell asleep as she explained to him that he had to change from white man's clothes. And the foolish white boy was so shy, he didn't want to take off his pants before this girl. She picked him up by his ears and shook him till the white man's pants fell off. Then she had to spank him to make him stay awake." She made as gentle a spanking motion as she could. "He screamed at being spanked. A scream so loud that a mile away a mountain lion hid in its cave from fear. He saw that the girl could see all of his naked body and blushed until his face, his ears, and even his white hair turned red, as red as it is today!" Then she walked over to Rusty and knocked off his hat and pulled his braids to her and hugged him, and made a bow to the crowd, as did Rusty, now blushing.

Later, in the lodge. "Hair turned white from fear and red from blushing. That was good. I should have thought of it. Hope you enjoyed, 'shy girl with no friends.'"

"Brother, it was a good story; the people liked it and will be talking about it for a while. I don't think father Tall Elk understood him as Little Fawn. Now that the whole village knows, I won't be able to make you blush about the spanking, will I?"

"I think the whole village always knew about it. How many did you tell? Not that it's important."

"I told no one except Mother when she asked why my hand was red. The next day some girls came to me and said people asked what was that smacking sound and yelling coming from our lodge. All I would say was, 'I can't say. Mother told me to tell no one.' But word spread. It's all past anyway. The important thing is that it made a good time for Burned Face and his bride. Good night, little brother with white hair turned red."

"Wait. I want your advice. I know a secret and should tell about it. There is a problem."

"If your secret is how you know what people say and think, I'm listening."

"The problem first. Father was in charge of cleaning up what the miners did to the creek so other miners won't stop there. From what I know about gold mining, there must be gold that the miners hid and was not found. I would have us look for it, to buy better guns, but it would not honor Father if gold that is hidden was found as he was in charge of the miners' camp after they were all shot. Should I talk to Father or go see if there is gold hidden? For if I am wrong, and they were poor miners, I don't have to tell. What do you think?"

"Don't think about going there. You know the Crow Black Knife wants you alive to torture. That is why you are not to leave the village without armed braves. There is no choice...talk to Father. This thought you have that there is gold hidden, is it really from your knowing about gold miners or from that magic you do that lets you know what people think and say?"

"No magic, just luck. When White Hawk and Twisted Nose killed the two miners, I and Burned Face were there. That is where Burned Face got the short shotgun. Those two miners were only working on the stream for a few days. The ones I tricked were many more men and worked longer. Yet only a little gold was found with their gear."

"What magic do you use to know how long they were there?"

Rusty laughed. "Burned Face taught me many tricks. All I had to do was to count the droppings from the horses to know how many days."

"I think you must tell our father. He will be here soon."

Tall Elk stuck his head into the lodge. "What are you two doing here? There is more dancing and storytelling."

While Rusty was slow to speak, Setting Sun was not. "Father, there is a something of importance that my brother would speak to you about."

"If there is, talk!" said Tall Elk in his usual brusque manner.

"Father, it is about the gold miners. I think it strange that for so many miners, working so many days, that we, the Cheyenne, found so little of their gold. The two miners that

30

Twisted Nose found last year had more gold in just a few days. There must be gold hidden that was not found. It would pay for many guns and powder. Do you think we should go and have a second look?"

"I will think on it. Chief Walks Fast is still at the fire. I will speak to him now. Late Setting Sun, there are many fine young braves hoping you will come back where they can see you tonight. But that is always your right. Son, we will talk in the morning."

"Rusty, here, I forgot, I have two things to show you. Cloud Woman made these." She took out some leather workings. First a narrow, highly decorated sheath for her Arkansas toothpick knife. It was a sheath that could be hidden in the pleats of a dress. Then two tapered sleeves of very stiff polished hide. "Put these on to see if they fit. This will protect your arm from the flash of the Colt rifle, so you can hold it the right way."

"Yes, this fits, but why two?"

"It would not look right to have one arm so covered and not the other. You should try it with the rifle in the morning. Good night, 'White hair blushed-red,'" she said while laughing.

Chapter 4

Tall Elk woke Rusty early. "Bring a rifle and come. We are going to look for hidden gold. Your pony is here and I have food for us."

Once mounted and joined by six braves, including White Hawk and Running Bear, Rusty spoke.

"I am pleased you are taking me. How is it, I, a boy of just barely fourteen summers, gets to ride with the best fighting braves? Is there a plan that I might have to speak as a marshal again?"

As usual, there was a pause before Tall Elk spoke. "Your words that we should look more for hidden gold were soon agreed to. As for your going, I told that you were as safe with us as at the village. The elders also said that if the gold was hidden by white men, a white man might be better able to think where it was. Without Sam with us, you are that white man."

A brave that had ridden ahead called them to rush to the place where the miners had been. When they reached that part of the stream, the brave was where the miners had their fort. He was pointing to horse droppings and telling how they were fresh. Others rode in a circle and reported back to Tall Elk who was in charge.

"Two men were hunting far from their fort when we attacked. They came back with a deer; part of it is over there. They saw that we had been here and the other miners were gone and they ran. They took only a leg of the deer. We are no more than one day's ride behind them," said Tall Elk to Rusty and White Hawk who was riding near Rusty.

"There are two men riding horses making deep hoof prints, riding to the southwest. They may be hoping to find a wagon train with many white men to protect them. The Bozeman wagon trail is four days' hard ride from here. Let us go," said White Hawk.

They would ride hard for a while, then walk for a spell and ride again. Rusty, like the rest, chewed on pemmican while walking. When a brave came back from the wrong direction, Rusty asked why.

"It is the best way. We ride as fast as we can, staying on the tracks they make. But two ride far ahead where they think the miners are going. If they find tracks, a signal is given and we can ride faster to that place since we don't have to track. If those going ahead find no signs, they must come back to us. It is a good way, and if this is a race, we are winning."

They were still riding as the sun began to set. The pace was now slower, but there was no stopping. The land was of gently rolling hills since they were within only a hundred miles of the eastern slop of the Rocky Mountains.

A brave that was far ahead of them waved an arm for them to come fast.

"We should now go together. I heard a shot!" he said. Tall Elk agreed.

Soon they saw that the riders they were after had changed directions and were now heading for high ground. Tall Elk looked to Rusty.

"They must have seen our dust and are fearful, as they should be."

Soon they came on a dead white man. He had been shot in the face. Next a lame horse was found. Rusty looked to Tall Elk to explain as they rode on.

"The tracks tell one horse went lame, for a short time they rode double. One of them got greedy or scared and shot the other for his horse and all the gold. Gold makes the heads of white men sick. We will catch him in the morning. It will be dark soon so we have no need to punish our horses now. His tracks tell that he is a heavy man or is carrying much gold. You were right to say we should do this. If he got away with that much gold, word would spread and the Cheyenne would be like a prairie dog town run over by a buffalo herd." Rusty saw Tall Elk smile at his comparison of Cheyenne to prairie dogs and white men gold seekers to buffalo.

They were riding together, the land was rolling low hills spaced a fourth to a half mile apart. The direction the white miner was taking soon had him in sight whenever he went over the top of a ridge when the Cheyenne were also on top.

The light was fading. With encouragement from the others, the pace was increased. As they started up a long incline, Tall Elk called for Rusty to give him his long rifle. Tall Elk called to the others that he should now lead. Just as Tall Elk reached a high point, he dismounted and knelt down. He used Rusty's rifle as one would use a stick to help him hold his rifle steady. Two hundred yards ahead, the miner came in sight as he topped the peak of a ridge. The cloud of smoke from a hundred grams of black powder hid the results of the shot for a second. Then the rider fell off his horse. There was yelling and whooping as the group rode up and took the horse. It was too tired to run.

"Look to the south," Tall Elk told Rusty. Far off there was a thin row of dust as far as the eye could see.

"Is that a wagon train? How far is that?" Rusty asked.

"It would not be over a half day's ride. The miner we caught did not see them in his fear. He could have made it to them if he was a Cheyenne." Tall Elk spoke with Running Bear and White Hawk. The man's gold, weapons and horse would be taken. Both men would be scalped and left to be

34

found as a warning. Nothing to show that they were gold miners would be left.

Rusty had some questions he saved till later when they made a camp and cooked a meal of fresh meat. It was horse meat. Rusty asked about the lame horse and the fact that the man who shot his companion left a good Colt pistol with the dead man.

"Good questions. That is how you are to learn. First the pistols. The man that was shot was left with a pistol because the man that shot him had two, one he was wearing and one in the saddlebags with the gold. It was there in case a person was making him give them gold. He must have been thinking he would reach into the bag for gold and come out with a pistol. And he was running with fear. The lame horse was not killed to save it from hurting, because we knew we might be back. We would not shoot it because of the sound of the shot. To cut its neck with a knife would send the smell of blood to bring wolves, or a bear. We are eating that meat now. I like horse meat. Is yours cooked enough? I know you like your meat more cooked than most braves."

The party stopped at the stream where the miners had left the dead deer.

"Here they are," cried Running Bear. He held up the two rifles that the miners had hidden.

Tall Elk explained to Rusty. "Those are heavy buffalo guns. The men left the guns because of the weight of gold and that they had to run for their lives. They should never had come here. Now we have their guns, horses, and gold we don't dare use."

"What of the pistols?" Rusty asked.

"Because I am a chief, I must set an example. There are five men, not including me, and you, a boy. The three pistols and two rifles will let each have a gun. I will give the horse to an old brave that has few ponies. The gold, the chiefs and elders will decide about. You are not to tell any that we have that gold. Even your friend, Sam Hiller, or your sister. Setting Sun will find out anyway...she always does."

Rusty learned that the chiefs and elders had decided to hold a small part of the gold to use to buy things from the whites on the wagon trains heading for Oregon. Most of the over sixty pounds of gold would be buried.

"Rusty, come, I want to show you something," said Red Falcon, a young brave.

"Will I need a rifle and pony?"

"Pony, yes. Need a rifle, no, but if I was you, I would never be without one. Come."

Rusty picked up his Colt rifle and the bag that carried powder and the .44 caliber lead balls. They rode a short distance to where several braves were waiting in tall grass. There on the ground was a dead Crow brave. He had a spear wound in his chest.

"See what weapon he carries. It is a war club, not a tomahawk, and he has no spear or bow." Red Falcon picked up the war club. It was made of hard wood with a large polished knot as a ball at one end.

"This is what I would use if I wanted to take a person as a prisoner. A few days ago we killed a Crow that had the same kind of weapon. And some have been chased away. They came not to steal horses. It is plain they were sent by the Crow chief, Black Knife, to take you, son of Tall Elk, for Black Knife to torture."

Rusty at first didn't know what to say.

"I thank you. I think it will be best if I stay close to the lodges, but I hate to show such fear. What would you have me do?"

"You have the ears of the chiefs. Help us talk them into letting us make a raid to punish the Crow. Many of us have not been as lucky as you and not counted coups as much."

This was what Rusty had longed for, a chance to gain the good feelings of the young braves.

"I would be pleased to ask for a raid, but I must do so with the request that I am to go." That statement was not liked by all. Rusty heard words like, "He is too young, he has only been lucky." He even read the lips of a brave that said, "Rusty will get in our way. He should let us use his rifle that shoots six times and stay and read to the girls." That made him mad, but there was nothing he could do without their knowing he could read lips.

There were times when Setting Sun even made her mother and father angry with her arrogance.

At the evening meal, she spoke. "The whole village knows that the chiefs are to bury gold. There is no way the place it is put will be kept a secret in this village of gossips. I have money in a bank. Could not the Cheyenne put gold in a bank?"

They all knew that her real father, Quinn, the Hudson Bay man who died, had told his brother in Ireland to look after his Indian daughter, and his brother had put money in a Quebec bank that she could have when she turned sixteen. She was now fifteen.

Tall Elk was not pleased but decided to set things straight.

"Yes, my know-it-all daughter. There is much gold. But it is to be buried with such a plan that it will be safe till we might need it. We chiefs worked out a good plan. For five days, five braves will ride out. One with the gold will stay in the center, but not where the others can see him. The four will cover all directions to make sure no one comes near him. On only one of the five trips will the gold be buried. On that trip the bags will come back loaded with sand. Only the one that hides the gold will know. He will only tell Chief Walks Fast and the Shaman Red Hatchet. It is a good plan. You are not to tell what I have said!"

Rusty told his father about his need to ask for a raid on the Crow.

"You have asked me, that is enough. I will speak to the elders."

"But Father, I promised the young braves that are protecting me from the anger of Black Knife that I would speak to the chiefs. I must not let them down. It is a good thing they asked me, since I have tried so hard to win their friendship."

"We chiefs have many problems. I will let you know when we might hear you. Prepare a strong speech, as you will have a hard time asking for a raid. It is not something to do without good reason."

Following the advice of Red Falcon, Rusty began to always carry a rifle. Most of the time it was the six-shot Colt. It was heavy, so many times he had it on his shoulder. He was teased about playing as a white man soldier. While waiting for Tall Elk to give him permission to speak for the raid, he would walk near the elders. One time from a distance he saw a dust covered brave speak to Chief Walks Fast. Rusty read his lips. He said, "There were three large rocks. I named them Father Bear, Mother Bear and Baby Bear. Two times a spear, towards the star that does not walk around, from the Baby Bear rock, deep, and well-covered with sod." Rusty walked away, worried that he now knew something he should not. The use of the three bears story had to come from the fairy tales he told on winter nights. The star that does not walk around would be the north star. This would bother him for days.

Rusty, frustrated that no one would hear him, was in a sad mood. He took his sling and went to practice.

When Rusty was bored the first weeks he was with the Cheyenne, he made an old world type of leather sling. It was different from the slings the Indians made and was far more accurate but harder to master. In time he made slings for his sister, Setting Sun, and her friend, Winter Rose. When he had free time he had started to practice. His favorite target was the three-inch lid of an old coffee pot hung from a tree. This day, like many, he was joined by boys much younger than he, and he would teach them. He was showing some boys how to use the sling when Setting Sun came with his and her javelins. Another of his things he had made because of his reading and thinking of ways to improve on Indian weapons. Setting Sun knew how good he was with the javelins and hoping to improve his mood, she joined him. Since he carried the Colt rifle, he was almost always wearing the hide wrist guard she had made for him. He was pleased to have her join him. He threw first one, then the other javelin, burying the long thin blades into the wood of a large cottonwood tree. Setting Sun went to gather more stones for the slings. She had hers with her. He left his rifle leaning on the tree from where he threw. That was what the two Crow braves were waiting for. They charged from the tall grass that had hidden their advance from the trees. Each had a war club. Rusty saw he was too far from his rifle. He pulled hard and the second javelin came free in time for him to step back, extend his throwing arm, and spear one of the Crow braves that was so close he could not duck but only put up a hide shield. The javelin went through it and into his chest. The second Crow was at him. Rusty had no time to throw, only jab with the second javelin and put up an arm to block the blow of the war club. The hide wrist guard helped block the club blow, and the Crow had to stop short because of the pointed javelin just touching his stomach. Then his head jerked to a side and he fell. Rusty turned to see Setting Sun putting a second stone in her sling. He stood over the first Crow and saw that it was not a fatal stab. The last thing he wanted was for this brave to live and be tortured. Rusty stuck him till he was dead. He checked and found the stone from Setting Sun was deep in the brave's temple. He was not breathing. Setting Sun ran for help in case there were more Crow and she wanted her best knife that she used to scalp the one she killed. Rusty sat against the tree, his rifle on his lap. He saw Tall Elk coming and started to rise, but when he pushed down with his left hand, it was painful. The hurt was a surprise. He began to remove the stiff hide wrist guard and the pain got worse. "I think my arm is broken!" he called to Setting Sun.

"Then don't remove the hide on your arm."

Soon, Tall Elk and others came and took him to the medicine man, White Weasel. He left saying that he was never going to be any more than arm's reach from a rifle. The arm was broken under the hide guard.

"What is this for? If it was to be a shield for your arm, it did not work."

"No, it is to protect my arm and wrist from the fire of my revolver Colt rifle. But I think it may have made the break less than it would have been."

White Weasel cut off Rusty's shirt sleeve and tightly wrapped his arm while Tall Elk and Setting Sun held his arm. After wrapping the arm with soft cloth, he put the wrist guard back and tied it on and hung his arm around his neck and tied it so Rusty could not move it.

"Come back when I send for you. I will have some green rawhide that I will make wet and wrap your broken arm with. Then it will dry and you will not be able to move the place that is broken. It will heal in two moons, if you don't try and use it. Be careful sleeping."

Rusty could do very little with a broken arm.

"You are lucky that you wore the hide on your arm. The Crow was trying to hit your head," said Cloud Woman.

Walking Dove suggested that he could read more stories while his arm healed. "Do you want me to get someone for you to read to?"

"Yes, in a day, when the wet rawhide gets more stiff, and this arm does not hurt as much."

Chapter 5

Sitting and doing nothing, he worried that he knew where the gold was buried. The idea made his heart beat faster when he thought about it. Was it right for him to know? Should he tell Tall Elk? He wished he had someone to ask for advice. He would do nothing about it for now. In preparing what he would say to the elders about a raid on the Crow, he thought about all the books he had read that told of battles. That, plus what his grandfather, who had fought in the Black Hawk Indian war, had told him, made him feel that he had good ideas about fighting. He was having trouble getting anyone to listen to his ideas.

"Burned Face, wait. Do you have time? I would like to tell you something." Burned Face was his best friend and two years older.

"I will let you speak as I ride to go watching the herd, but you can only go so far from the lodges, it is said."

"Thank you. You are a true friend. The many books I have read tell about fighting, not in the way of the Indians. All Indians, including we Cheyenne, want to fight as a single person. We fight to win glory, to count coups. But the white man's army fights as a team. They stay together and fire many times at one enemy. We could learn from them. I have plans. I need to talk to the warriors, but none will listen to me. I can save lives!" he said as his friend rode off, waving him back.

Rusty asked his father, Tall Elk, when could he speak about the raid and fighting to the elders and war chiefs. He was told he did not have to speak on it.

"It has been agreed, the Crow have become a problem and need to be punished. You do me a dishonor going around speaking as if you know more about fighting than the great warriors in our village. Go and find your sister, Setting Sun. I have news for her."

His mother, Walking Dove, saw his need and asked if she could help.

"Would you? If I could get you and Berry Woman, the wife of Chief Walks Fast, to hear me tell my information..., my battle plan, and maybe you could get a brave to also listen to me, I know I can make our Cheyenne warriors fight better. You would know if I was speaking true words."

Berry Woman was fond of Rusty. Ever since he had joined the tribe, he would some evenings read books and tell stories to the squaws, and once he read some newspapers to them.

With the help of Berry Woman and over the objection of Tall Elk, Rusty got his chance to speak about warfare. Berry Woman sent for Rusty and Walking Dove while Chief Walks Fast was away visiting the Sioux. They gathered in the chief's big lodge. There were two very old braves, ones that no longer hunted or went on the war parties. They were jokingly called The Fat Bellies. Rusty saw that one came with a war bonnet of many feathers.

Rusty smoothed the dirt and began to put down many little sticks. He had to move slowly with his arm still in a tight wrap of rawhide and tied to his chest.

First he arranged some sticks all spread out over a large area and pointing one way. Opposite those sticks he made a line of sticks with a space between them, then a back line where the spaces were. He pointed to his sticks as he spoke.

"The Cheyenne and all Indians go to war looking for glory and honor first, killing the enemy second. As is the case with coup sticks. The white man does not have coup sticks; he uses guns. The Cheyenne fight as one man against one enemy. The white man's army fights as many against one. See these sticks as soldiers?" He pointed to the twin rows. "The front row fires. They are protected by the back row while they reload their guns, then the back row fires, protected by the front row."

He was interrupted by an older brave who said, "The soldiers all have rifles, many of our braves have rifle guns, but it is less than half of them. And it is hard to load a long rifle while fighting on horse."

"I did not say to fight on horse!" This remark drew a stern look from Walking Dove, a look that said he was with his elders and should be careful about being respectful.

"Yes, you are right. The pony soldiers stop, get off their ponies to fight. Look here." He held his hands as if holding a rifle while riding. It jumped around and was hard to aim. Then he pretended to get off a horse and kneel and hold the rifle steady. "You are right about not all of our warriors having rifles. But we have more rifles than the Crow, thanks to our friend Sam Hiller. Think of a fight where our braves advance in a kind of row, braves next to each other taking turns using rifles and arrows. The arrows used while the brave on your side is reloading his rifle. This is the way to kill Crow. Coups can be best counted on dead Crow! That is all I can say. I could make a demonstration if some braves would help me." He saw a look from Walking Dove. "I thank you for giving me this time and hearing what a...lost white boy, now a Cheyenne, has to say."

Rusty walked back to his lodge dreaming of doing a demonstration using many braves. He would have them use blank loads and blunted arrows. Maybe he would recreate the famous battle of Cannas when Hannibal defeated the

Roman legions with a refused center and an entrapment move.

No one spoke to him the rest of the day or the next about his talk. He was sure he had made no one change how they would fight. Over two weeks passed and there was no news about any raid. His arm was healing. He grew bored and was reading the Bible when he found some interesting stories. He surprised his family one morning when he said, "I want to read a story to just my family. May I do so after last meal?"

Later, when they were all sitting, he took out the Bible and read the story of David and Goliath. He told how there was a war, and in those olden times one brave could challenge a single brave from the other tribe and all would watch. He told of the great warrior that was as large as any two men and had a shield few men could pick up. And all feared him. When no brave would fight him, a small girl came and said she would use her sling and kill him just as she had killed a lion.

When this girl came with only a sling, the big brave Goliath said, "Am I only a dog to be chased away with stones?" And the small girl put a stone in her sling and slung it into his forehead and he fell. She had no knife so she used his to cut off his head; his knife was so large she had to use both hands.

"I tell you that story because of my sister saving my life a second time, first with only a fishing spear, and then with a sling and small stone, just as David killed Goliath long before years were counted, and in a land far away. I read this story as a way to thank her." All were pleased, and Setting Sun made him promise to read it to her friends.

"Yes, on the first day when it rains," he said.

Walking Dove told him that Walks Fast had returned from speaking with the Sioux. "It took him a while, but if there is a raid, he will have many Sioux joining this clan of Cheyenne."

Setting Sun called him to come back to the lodge when she saw him walking.

"I see your arm is no longer broke. Is your six-shot rifle clean and has it oil? Do you know which pony you plan to ride?" She had that smile of hers when she knew something he didn't.

He wondered what were her ways of always knowing what was going on. "What are you talking about, please?"

"Very well, great master general of making war. The braves that will raid the Crow are leaving in the morning at first light. Walks Fast has returned. Many Sioux will join us, in trade for some of the Crow horses and captured rifles. We will ride out with them. That is all I can say."

He grabbed her and was about to kiss her when she hooked her foot behind his and tripped him. She smiled and looked down at him. "Don't bother with making war paint. And that is all I can tell you. Tall Elk has said so."

Rusty could not sleep in anticipation of being in a great battle. The first thing he saw at dawn was Cloud Woman removing a double barrel shotgun from a hiding place. Tall Elk was instructing Walking Dove in the use of a Colt .44 pistol, like the ones they had taken from the miners. He saw Cloud Woman load her gun; it was an old flintlock. She was carefully measuring the gunpowder and then, after a wading from a paper wasp nest, she counted out a load of big buckshot into each barrel.

"Mother Cloud Woman, I never saw that gun. It is of the old type that does not always fire. I will leave you my Hawkins rifle when I go to fight the Crow."

The adults looked at each other, then to a waking Setting Sun. Tall Elk spoke.

"Daughter, did I not tell you to talk to your brother about where you two are going and what you are to bring here?"

"I must not have made my words clear. Sorry, Father."

"Rusty, my brother, we are only riding out with the war party for a short ways. Then we go east to a Mandan village to try and bring back a white man, a missionary who is a teacher. Our mothers are being armed to protect themselves if Crow come looking for you."

"You should bring your six-shot rifle. The Hawkins can be left if you wish. Setting Sun may bring her pistol." Then as a joke, Tall Elk said, "You should not worry about your two mothers—they fight so fierce that if they went on the Crow raid, we could leave half our braves free to go and fish." His mood changed when he saw how disappointed Rusty was. He looked to Setting Sun.

"I told you not to let word of where you are going be spread in the village. That did not mean you had the right to make your brother think he was going on a raid. A raid you know has been on his mind for days. When will you get over not treating him as a girl should treat her brother?" He looked at Rusty who had dropped the rifle balls he was putting into a small bag.

"And you, my son, is your head so full from books that you think Cheyenne warriors would let a boy of thirteen summers tell them about war, and fighting?"

Walking Dove saw how crestfallen Rusty was and spoke. "Yes, my wise chief of a husband, but is it not true that for days braves have argued over the fighting ideas of our son. And have not a few braves made plans to try some of what he said when Falling Beaver spoke to them."

"Who is Falling Beaver?" asked Rusty.

"He is one of the Fat Bellies you spoke to at the lodge of Walks Fast when Berry Woman and our mother let you speak," said Setting Sun.

No one spoke. It was so rare for Walking Dove to challenge Tall Elk around the children.

Cloud Woman broke the ice by showing her shotgun to Rusty. "See the notches in the stock? Half were from kills of my father, Breaks Bones, and these I put here. Most after Tall Elk and I were married." Cloud Woman pointed to six notches cut in the stock.

"Let us eat. It will be pemmican for days," said Tall Elk, as he pointed to a steaming pot.

Rusty excused himself and went to make water. He saw that his best pony was already tied with two others nearby. He took a deep breath and returned with plans to make the best he could of his fate.

Since it was a three-day ride to the Crow village, the Cheyenne carried their war paint to apply later. One half of a day's ride out and the direction was changed for Rusty, Setting Sun and the braves Gray Wolf, Running Antelope and an older brave, Red Fox. While the young braves, Gray Wolf and Running Antelope, said they would rather be with the war party going after the Crow, Rusty was sure it was a chance to impress Setting Sun that led them into making this trip.

For the first day and night, they made no fire and ate pemmican. Then when it was believed they were beyond danger of meeting any Crow or Pawnee, game was shot, but with arrows. There was an evening cooking fire. At first the two young braves told all about their great deeds as they tried to impress Setting Sun. When Rusty could take no more, nor could the mature Red Fox, Red Fox asked Rusty about his ideas on how to wage war. Rusty had to defend his criticisms of the Indian way of fighting as individuals versus the white man's group organized way. In time, they began to see the merits of what Rusty was saying. Rusty expressed his disappointment that he could not go on the raid. He was surprised when Running Antelope told him that he should think of his being on that raid, because several of the young braves were planning to fight in teams of two or three. They would be trying to use both the method that Rusty had suggested and the traditional Indian ways.

The second night while Rusty and Setting Sun were away and the raid on the Crows was en route, a small party of Crow warriors came to steal horses and/or take Rusty captive. Cloud woman had tied a dog inside the lodge and it gave a warning growl when three Crow braves tried to enter the lodge. Cloud Woman shot one with her shotgun and Walking Dove shot a second, shooting right through the side of the lodge at his outline. The dog was turned loose and it bit the leg of a Crow, holding him and making it possible for Walking Dove to shoot him with the pistol. The shooting made the village alarmed and halted the attempt to steal horses. The Crow brave bit by the dog and shot with the pistol did not die until he was tortured for two days.

Chapter 6

On the high prairie, the party going to the Mandan village had to hide from a passing column of Blue U.S. Army Cavalry.

At the Mandan village they met with the Reverend Anthony J. Thomas, a man so pious that Rusty began to wonder if this was a good idea. Setting Sun explained that she was given permission from their chief and the elders to invite him to come and stay in their village, if he would run a school. He would be allowed to do missionary duties and try to convert to Christianity as long as his work did not interfere with the harmony of the tribe and his school taught the tribe's children, like they do in a white man's school. Rusty would learn the whole idea was Setting Sun's.

The Mandan village was poor when compared to the Cheyenne's village. The Reverend Thomas decided he had to think about moving and would either come in one moon or not. Rusty was able to speak with some of the Mandan and learned that this man of God was always complaining about things, like how the Indians dressed, and he was against all wars and killing, except for game to eat. The Mandan told Rusty this man of God ate too much and was hard to please. They left with no clear word if he would come or not.

Gray Wolf was the first to see them. "Look, two Pawnee riding slow towards us. They are holding a bundle. I can't tell what it is. They are making peaceful signs. What should we do?"

49

Red Fox said they should meet with them, with guns ready.

They rode up. There were just the two Pawnee and what they were holding was a small white boy. Rusty understood enough of their language to serve as an interpreter.

"They say this boy was lost from a wagon train, and they found him. Would we like to trade for him? They don't want him, he cries a lot."

Red Fox said, "Ask what they plan to do with the boy, if we don't trade for him?"

"They say he will be left on the trail used by the white man's wagons. They are tired of his crying."

"If they leave him alone, wolves will eat him," said Setting Sun.

"If I say we trade for him, will the daughter of Tall Elk find a lodge that would take such a boy of so little value?"

"I will say that," said Setting Sun.

"Then what have you to trade?" asked Red Fox.

Rusty broke the silence. "Here, I have this fine Bowie knife." With a nod of approval from Red Fox, Rusty handed over his new Bowie knife to a Pawnee brave.

"See, it cuts both ways," he said while pointing to the top third of the blade.

The Pawnee that took the knife spoke to the other and that brave set the boy on the ground. They rode off looking back at the armed Cheyenne till they were out of rifle range.

Setting Sun picked up the small boy and put him before her on her pony. She tried talking to him, but it was clear he could not understand her. For a while after she picked him up, he did not cry. Rusty tried English and what few words of German he remembered from his mother. This started the boy crying again. He never stopped either crying or whimpering, except when eating or relieving himself, which he had to do many times. Setting Sun soon learned that when a couple of hours passed and the boy began to wiggle, she had to stop for him to pee.

It was mid-day when they reached the village. The boy was all but forgotten about. At first Walking Dove told of the fight with Crows that she and Cloud Woman had won. Then reports of the raid began. The boy went right to sleep when put in their lodge. There was only a brief explanation from Setting Sun about the boy.

The raiding party had returned that morning. The raid was a huge success. Only two Cheyenne braves were killed, five more were wounded, all with minor wounds. And they had many scalps from the Crow. The village Crier came with a message to Rusty that he was to go and see Chief Walks Fast. It was an honor to have the Crier deliver such a message.

Rusty ran, then slowed to a steady, more dignified walk, as he reached the lodge of Chief Walks Fast. His father, Tall Elk, was there as was his uncle, Twisted Nose, and other important warriors like White Hawk and Running Bear. Walks Fast spoke. Thirteen-year-old Rusty stood as if at attention like soldiers do and listened.

"Dreams A Lot. There are words I would have you hear before the council fire later today. You have made your father proud with the book words about fighting that you shared with the Cheyenne. Some of your words were used, that will be talked of tonight. I wanted you to hear that praise from me. You are here because...you have become a good Cheyenne brave in dress and learning our words and how we believe. You have proved to be brave and...can think of good ways to do things. There is one part of being a Cheyenne where we think you may be weak." He touched his heart. "You can kill in battle, but have soft heart about the torture of enemies. You are to be given a chance to prove that is no longer so, because you may have private reasons to do your Cheyenne duty to an important captive, and as a reward for the words you gave to our young bucks about how to fight, you are to take charge and do the torture of...Black Knife of the Crow. Remember, his screams bring comfort to the widows of the Cheyenne braves that were killed and to the wounded."

Tall Elk walked Rusty back to their lodge, speaking on the way. "Son, this Crow, Black Knife, wanted to torture you. He will be a hard man to make scream. Get advice from Cloud Woman and maybe use your good head. Do not fail me in this. Now what is this I hear about a strange little boy that cries a lot?"

* * * * * *

The Cheyenne did not know the little boy was Polish. He had run after a puppy when Pawnee braves came to steal horses from their wagon train heading west and he was left behind. He spoke no English and had been warned about Indians that would scalp and kill him. He was just barely five years old and it was only two months since his getting off a ship where he had been sick all the time. For now, his name was Cry A Lot. Tall Elk and Walking Dove were pleased that Setting Sun had shown an interest in the boy and that Rusty had given up his new best knife to save an innocent life. Tall Elk asked Setting Sun, "What are you going to do with this boy that cries all the time? If he is to stay here, you must fix that."

"I don't know. There must be a lodge that would like to raise a boy. He looks in good health. No one knows what he is saying, but that is not important, since he must learn Cheyenne. May I ask at the council fire this evening when the whole village is there to learn about the raid on the Crow?"

"I will think on it. What is your news about the man of God that teaches, the missionary at the Mandan village?"

"He did not say. He wants to think about coming here. You should ask my brother about that man. He talked to some Mandans about him."

"Rusty, what can you tell me about this?"

"Some I spoke with liked him as a good man. Others said he does not understand Indian ways and was so pious..., he...it is hard for me to say...he is so much a man of God that he could be a problem. He tells people things that are not about his faith. I can't say to have him here or not. He is said to be a learned man with books. And should be a good teacher, if he wants to be."

"What kind of things do the Mandan complain about this holy man?"

"They say he does not like...no..., he gets...angry when he sees anyone that is not covering his or her body. Even little children running naked, he chases with a stick away from where he is. That is all I can say. I must prepare for my duty to torture Black Knife."

When Tall Elk left, Rusty spoke to Cloud Woman. "Tell me, did you use your old time shotgun to defend this lodge?"

"Yes, my gun made a hole in a Crow you could stick your arm in and not get blood on it. Your mother, Walking Dove, shot one with Tall Elk's pistol and one with your long rifle. The Crow she shot with the pistol was not lucky. He did not die for two days. His screams were so that mothers said it stopped their milk and asked me to make him dead." She laughed at the last remark.

"How should I do Black Knife? My head is open for advice."

"There are some rules you should know. For an important man like this Crow, it would be wrong to blind him so he would not see in the next world. It is in bad taste to cut off his male parts, even if the Bluecoat soldiers do that to Indians. Fire hurts more on some parts, like hands, feet and under arms. Remember the threat is sometimes as useful as the real. Fake to cut many times before cutting. He must be made to last more than one day. After you have done some things, it would be right for you to get help. That help should first come from family of killed Cheyenne, then from their friends. You should tell them about that before."

Rusty went for a walk. Children were gathering much wood for a big fire. He saw he was near the lodge of Iron Hand, the arrow maker, and remembered the Bowie knife he had traded. He wanted to get the torturing off his mind.

"Greetings, Iron Hand, my teacher. I will need to make a new Bowie knife. Do you have any more of the good steel we used to make it?"

"Yes, but look here." He removed a skin and there were several Bowie knives just like the one Rusty had traded. "Here, take one."

Rusty picked one up. "Only until I return the gift."

"It would not be right for you to not have what you showed us to make. Think no thought about a return gift for a thing like that knife. I hear you have the honor of making your enemy feel the pain of making war on the Cheyenne. Can I help?"

"Yes, please. I don't know much. I have never done that before. I only hope I don't make a fool of my family by puking when I torture him."

"Will any of these help?" Iron Hand asked as he lifted some branding irons.

"Yes, let's see." Rusty found one that was the letter 'C' with a line over it and a second that had a plain tip. The kind called a running iron, used to change brands or write with.

"This will do. I'm sure there will be a fire to heat them with. Thank you. I must walk and think what I am to say."

"Wait, my red haired young friend. A word of advice. Don't eat a lot tonight if you think your stomach might be weak. You will do good, use your good head, be different."

Rusty took the branding iron and walked to think. He found he was behind the lodge of Walks Fast. A group of young braves were there. When he got near them, Burned Face called to him.

"Here is Black Knife. Come, make him fear you."

Rusty saw that on the ground tied to a pole was an adult Crow brave. His one leg was hanging by a thin bit of skin. His knee had been almost blown away.

"This looks like the work of your short shotgun. Did my friend shoot this Crow?"

Others patted Burned Face on his back.

"Yes," said Red Falcon. Burned Face says he shot there to help us catch this Crow. Before the battle while we put on war paint, White Hawk told us we should try to get this man alive or dead. I think it was a lucky miss. Burned Face says his shot to the leg was a thing he tried to do. We are grateful for the words you said about how to fight. When a few of us fought in pairs and were doing good, others did the same. Only the wild old warriors like Running Bear did their fighting alone. He ran down many Crow that tried to run. You should look at the new scalps on his lance. He may have to get a longer lance."

"Now tell this old woman of a Crow what you have for him," said Burned Face.

Rusty saw he had no choice. He took one of the branding irons and used it to lift the lowered chin of Black Knife. He spoke in the language of the Crow to Black Knife, and in Cheyenne for the braves guarding him.

"See this? Do you know what it is? It is a white man's branding iron. He makes it hot and burns his cattle with his name. You will go to the next world wearing a 'C' for the Cheyenne on your skin where all can see. But you will be blind and can't see them." When a brave said, "You should not blind him," Rusty yelled a war whoop to drown out his words. Then in a whisper, he explained that he knew the rules about blinding. "I plan to make this dog meat think I will take out his eyes because I, as not a true Cheyenne, would not know any better." There was smiling and nodding in agreement with what Rusty said.

Rusty was walking back to his lodge when he heard loud crying and saw the boy they had traded for being hit with sticks and chased by village children. He forced his way into a group that had the boy on the ground and were kicking him. Rusty picked up the boy and made them back off. He carried the dirty, whimpering boy to their lodge. Cloud Woman saw him and the shape the boy was in.

"I could get no cooking done with the noise he was making. I put him out. When Setting Sun comes back, she is to learn that the boy is hers to deal with."

Setting Sun did not return. She sent Winter Rose to get her best dress and say that she was eating with Winter Rose and White Hawk. Cloud Woman objected and refused to let Winter Rose take the dress. "Tell Late Setting Sun she is to come here now!" said Cloud Woman.

Rusty stopped Winter Rose. "When you come to the council fire, bring your sling that I taught you to use." Walking Dove and Tall Elk returned to eat and change for the evening of speeches and the torture of Black Knife. The little boy for now named Cry A Lot was in a corner living up to his name. Cloud Woman spoke to them about Setting Sun and the boy she had returned with. Rusty heard a word about Setting Sun he had never heard before and asked Walking Dove in English what it meant.

"It is used to say a person is always mischievous. And that is my daughter."

Setting Sun returned. The expression on her face was such that she did not need to say she was not happy about being ordered to return to the family lodge. Rusty expected Cloud Woman or Walking Dove to say they were displeased with her because of the crying boy. Instead, Cloud Woman spoke in a calm voice.

"Setting Sun, don't you know how to ask for help? There are some older squaws that for a small gift would take in this crying boy until you know what to do with him. You are not the only one that will be taking part this evening at the council fire. All of this lodge is expected to be there. Would you like me to find somebody to watch your new brother?" There was a pause when she said "new brother." Before any could question, she laughed and said she was joking about the boy. She looked at Rusty and said, "You did not cry but only half as much as this outcast your sister has dragged in."

Tall Elk spoke first. "Yes, first wife, please find a person to watch this boy for a few days."

Walking Dove then added, "I will supply whatever gifts to take to have that done. My ears are sore from his crying."

Rusty spoke, with a laughing voice. "But Cloud Woman, did I truly cry in the night more than four nights out of five nights?"

"No, brother, it was maybe one night in every two moons. Are you thinking of the crying you did in your head for the freckles that you have lost?"

"Setting Sun, I would speak to you." He had her step out of the lodge. "I wish you to bring your sling. If I ask as a part of the torture, could you and Winter Rose hit this Crow, Black Knife, with stones, hard, if I explain it as a part of the torture?"

"Yes, we would. Will you bring the stones?"

"I don't have time. Is there a young brave that would be glad to bring some as a favor for the two most desirable Cheyenne maidens? Could you ask one to bring a bag of the right size stones? We would only need about three dozen." He was glad Setting Sun understood English and numbers. It was awkward using the Indian way, where he would have to say something like number of fingers three times.

Rusty went to the braves watching Black Knife and asked them that he be tied on the stake using a cross pole so that his open palms be facing to the front and his arms extended just above the shoulders to expose the arm pits. He was assured it would be done so.

All afternoon there was wailing and crying from squaws over the braves that had died during the raid. A stake was put in the ground in the middle of the council meeting area. The biggest fire Rusty had ever seen was laid out. He placed his two branding irons next to the fire. There were extra piles of wood nearby. Drums were beaten and the Cheyenne people began to sit on blankets, except for those that danced.

Red Hatchet, the Shaman, made the first speech and blew smoke towards all the braves that took part in the raid. They stood in one group. Rusty was placed next to Walking Dove because Tall Elk was with the raider group. The Shaman praised the fighting spirits and thanked the ancestors of fighting Cheyenne braves that had watched over them in battle. Chief Walks Fast spoke next after he described the brave fighting men, naming all of them. He pointed to Rusty. who was shocked when he heard his name called.

"I show you the son of Tall Elk, the brave Dreams A Lot...Rusty, who was not on this great, successful raid, but his words were there. He gave to our young braves wisdom about fighting that he says came from white man's books, but I know came from a wise Cheyenne medicine man that must have spoken to him as a wolf-dog during his vision quest. He has been a teacher to some of our tribe, now I ask him to be a teacher to the Crow, Black Knife, and make him sing with sorrow that he ever came at the Cheyenne."

Rusty looked for direction and was pointed to the stake where Black Knife, the Crow, was tied in the manner Rusty had asked.

He knew he had to make a speech, and that helped him set his mind to what he was going to do. Ever since he had been told that he must be the main torturer, he had strained to set aside any Christian values.

After he had made a series of thank you's for the braves, chiefs and all, he addressed the Crow, Black Knife. This was different. He spoke to the tied warrior in his own language and then repeated in Cheyenne to the crowd what he said. Then he called for his sister, Late Setting Sun, and Winter Rose to come forward.

"Over a year ago, these fine Cheyenne maidens," he didn't like to use squaws, "were almost taken by two Crow braves. With good luck and help from my sister, we killed those two Crow. One was the son of this Crow, Black Knife. He has tried to take me and torture me because I killed his son. You know what fate was waiting for these fine Cheyenne maidens. That is why I ask them to start this making a Crow sing." He pulled out his sling, put in a stone the size of a bird's egg, swinging it around and letting it fly to strike the Crow in his chest. He jumped, not crying out, but shocked at the force of the hit. Then both girls began to take turns hitting him with stones from their slings. There were cheers from the people at the sound of these hits. Setting Sun whispered to Winter Rose and a contest began. From the hit in the belly, Setting Sun began to hit in a downward line hits an inch apart. Winter Rose started in mid-thigh and began to walk her way up with strikes that left deep red marks. The cheers grew louder as the girls closed in on his male glands that were lightly covered by;.. a scrap, of deerskin. Rusty could see Black Knife sweat. His arm bled where he fought the rawhide that tied him. Then he screamed for the first time as a stone hit his most tender part. There was a great cheer. It looked like he might faint, so Rusty told the girls to end it.

"We have only a few stones left," said Setting Sun, as she hit his hand with a well-aimed and very hard strike. Winter Rose hit the other hand. You could hear bones break. They stopped to cheers and clapping. Rusty heard encouragement for making a good start. Before she left, he asked for and took Setting Sun's long knife, the Arkansas toothpick. He had asked her to bring it. He had been heating the branding irons. *This is going to be the hard part; I must not fail*, he thought. Holding a hot iron, he addressed the Crow in a voice all could hear.

"When you get to the after world, all will know who sent you." He put the red hot branding iron on the open hand. It burned in a letter C. He held up the iron. "This is the white man's letter 'C', a C like in Cheyenne." Then he burned the other hand, and was holding it to the flesh of the chest when the Crow began to scream.

Black Knife began to sing his death song. He looked at Rusty and spoke to himself without voicing out loud. *I will get you with my knife in the next life. I will never forget, white boy!* He did not know Rusty could read his lips. Next Rusty took the long thin knife and pointed it at the Crow. He walked ever so slowly to the Crow with the knife pointed right at the left eye. There was a look of hate and fear in the eyes of Black Knife. Rusty was glad he was not looking down and wondered if the people could see his nervously shaking knees. *Now is when I have to do my best acting,* he thought. The knife was within an inch of the eye when he spoke in a whisper in the language of the Crow.

"You will not see anyone in the next life. Your knife won't be able to find this white boy when I cut out your eyes." At that, Black Knife screamed with a fear that impressed the crowd. Rusty closed his own eyes and pushed the knife slowly till he felt it touch an eye, then he backed it out. Black Knife had blinked and there was only a small red dot of blood on the eyelid. Black Knife began to sing his death song again. Rusty took the knife and cut into Black Knife's chest. A drawing of a large finger with a smaller finger making taps on it. The Plains Indians' sign for Cheyenne. When Rusty stepped back for all to see, there was a cheer. He took the red hot running iron and traced over the cuts. Then he spoke. "Now this Crow will go to his next life with all to know that the Cheyenne sent him there." He stepped back and held up the long bloody knife. "Is there any here that feels they have the right to stick this Crow? Let them come here now." A line soon formed. Walks Fast called out that this Crow must be alive for another day of torture. "Not to cut deep!" he said. A squaw cut off the leg that was hanging by a thin piece of skin and threw it in the fire. That brought a cheer and remarks about Black Knife hopping on one leg in the next world.

Rusty would have given anything for a chair. Walking Dove must have seen his weak knees, for she came and hugged him and led him to Tall Elk. Even Setting Sun came and told him he had made the tribe proud. She stood so close that she braced him between herself and Walking Dove. The Crow had many small cuts, and became a figure covered with blood when Walks Fast sent a brave to take the knife and stop the cutting. The knife was returned to Rusty who gave it back to Setting Sun. Two squaws went up and rubbed dirt into the cuts to stop the bleeding and increase the pain. *Rusty wondered if he could stand a second day like this.* "I have to!" he said out loud and then saw Setting Sun look and ask if he was well?

He was able to sit when the many long speeches about the raid began. He listened carefully for clues of how the fighting was done. He was not disappointed to hear many times braves tell of fighting in the manner that the son of Tall Elk had suggested. He learned that one time Tall Elk killed a famous Crow war chief in single combat and that caused him to be attacked by four Crow braves. The men with rifles shot two of the four, he crushed the head of one and scared the other away, where that one was hit by an arrow. After the battle, when there was scalping, White Hawk insisted the scalp of the Crow that Tall Elk scared should go to Tall Elk with the scalp of the others. It was a one-sided fight, with the Crow on the losing side to well-armed Cheyenne and the many Sioux. The Crow village was burned and the surviving Crow left to run to the woods. A few captive small boys were kept by the Sioux to be given to lodges that had lost children to sickness. The Crow horses had been scattered. Those taken were divided with the Sioux. Two Sioux chiefs were present to be honored.

Rusty was still upset about the torturing. He had a hard time believing he had done that to another living being. *How will I get through a second day of looking into the eyes of Black Knife,* he thought. The speech making and retelling of the fighting went on and on.

He looked for Tall Elk, but could not see him. "Mother Walking Dove, would it be a problem for the family if I went to our lodge? I want to think and plan for tomorrow?"

"Setting Sun, walk your brother back to the lodge."

"I am not an old tired man. Let go of my arm, sister."

"Just trying to be helpful. I know this has been a hard day for you. It is hard to torture for a first time, the next two days will be easier."

"Two days! Do you think he can live that long?"

"It is up to you. Would you like a suggestion? I have seen more of this than you would have in your white man's world."

"As a part of the next day's torture, you could have some young braves shoot him with arrows, trying to stick but not hit the places that would kill him. I could help you ask them. There are many that would like to do that."

"Yes, ask some braves to shoot arrows. Now I want to close my eyes and sleep and not think." They had reached the lodge.

"Wait, there is a question. Many were worried that you were going to blind Black Knife. Cloud Woman told me she advised you not to do that. Did you forget what she said?"

"No, but I have made Black Knife believe I am going to cut out his eyes. That is part of my plan to give him fear. I have him thinking that because I am...was a white man, I will not follow the rules. I will not blind him. Now let me sleep, the night is almost over, it will be light soon."

"A good plan to make him fear you. I will tell Father and he will tell Walks Fast that you are not going to take out Black Knife's eyes, only make him think you are."

Rusty was right. The evening activities had lasted to within an hour of first light. The rest of the family returned to find Rusty sleeping fully dressed, not in the old cotton shirt he liked to wear at night.

"Help me undress him. These beaded clothes of his are not for sleeping," Walking Dove said to Setting Sun."

"Yes, Mother, but if he wakes up and sees it is me taking off his clothes, he will blush and will be unhappy with me," said Setting Sun.

"He will not wake up, to be sure, we will not try and put on his sleeping shirt." He did not wake.

* * * * * *

In the shadow of the lodge of Walks Fast, near where Black Knife was tied, no longer tied standing but in a sitting position, was a young squaw. She was waiting for the single guard of Black Knife to walk off, maybe to relieve himself. Her name was Little Blackbird. She was half Blackfoot and half Crow. She was a captive second wife of one of the Cheyenne braves that had died during the raid. Her arms were bloody from many small cuts and she had ashes in her hair and on her face from her mourning. Her fate was in the hands of Chief Walks Fast. She feared what brave she would be given to. As a captive second squaw, she faced years of hard work. Her heart went out to Black Knife. She had heard his death song as he was tortured and heard his cries that it was not right for him to go to the next life blind. When the brave guarding Black Knife walked away to some bushes, she moved in fast, putting a hand over Black Knife's mouth. She pointed to her knife and his throat. He nodded and when her hand was removed, he thanked her in a whisper saying, "Yes, thank you, and the good spirit that sent you." He leaned his head back and she cut open the side of his neck and walked away softly. Then she ran. Black Knife leaned his head to hide the heavily bleeding cut. He was dead when the sun came up a short time later. Tall Calf, who was the guard, studied the footprints and drew a circle with his knife around the ones of Little Blackbird and sent for help. It was not long till they knew who had helped Black Knife escape his final torture. A very angry Walks Fast picked four hot-tempered young bucks to go after the girl. Their only instructions were, "She must not reach any Crow. Do with her as you please."

Rusty woke to see Setting Sun and Cloud Woman eating. Sun quickly jumped on his hide covering. "Before you rise, my brother, I must warn you to check what you are wearing," she said with a giggle. He lifted the elk skin and saw he was wearing nothing.

"Did you undress me?"

"Oh, no! It would not be proper for a sister to undress a brother of your age. I had Winter Rose, Voice Like A Man and another girl do the undressing."

Cloud Woman laughed and said, "Your sister is teasing. Your mothers undressed you to make you sleep better. Setting Sun was not here."

"I have news you will like and some you might not like. Put on some clothes while we look away with our eating," said Setting Sun.

"What news? If it is truly good, I would like to hear it. I slept poorly and it was a short night."

"You will not be torturing Black Knife. His throat was cut during the night by Little Blackbird, the half Crow. She has run and some braves have gone after her. She may wish she had cut her own throat if they catch her."

"Say no more of that. We are eating," spoke Cloud Woman.

Rusty dressed and joined them. Cloud Woman reminded him to speak softly as others were still sleeping.

"What is the bad news? Now I can take it." Rusty felt like a great weight was lifted off him. His only plan was to take Sun's advice and have arrows shot into Black Knife and hope one brave would miss and put one in his heart.

"We are to have the boy, Cry A Lot back. No one else can stand him. He talks with funny words none can understand when he is not crying or whining. He is not much of a boy."

"You are the one that said to bring him, I remind you. So he is yours. You can practice being a mother with him," said a much relieved Rusty. "I am going to the stream to bathe. I smell of death and burned skin."

"You may be still very tired and weak. Last night you could not even stand. Shall I get some of my friends to help you wash your back side?" joked Setting Sun.

"I am in such a good mood I don't even mind your poor efforts at teasing. Sure, bring them all, I can give each girl a freckle to wash."

"We don't have that many girls in the whole Cheyenne nation! Yes, you do smell of burned skin. Go make yourself clean. There are to be more speeches today. Only half the braves have told of their deeds. And Sly Fox and Berry Woman have asked your father to make sure you are well and will be there today."

"Help me. Who is Sly Fox?"

"He is one of the Fat Bellies that you spoke to at the lodge of Walks Fast. You should thank him for telling that your ways to fight would work. He was the first to talk some braves into trying out your ideas. They used blank loads in rifles and tested your ideas in fake fighting on the way to the Crow village."

Rusty was done washing at the stream when he heard Setting Sun call out. "May I come? Are you dressed?"

"Yes, come over here by the willows." He was planning to say that her calling out was a step towards her becoming a better sister with, 'Before you would not have called to catch me without clothes to make me blush.' He didn't get to say anything. The boy that cried came running to the stream chased by Setting Sun who caught him when he had to stop at the water.

"They brought him back and he smells. He soiled his pants. Cloud Woman gave me the job of cleaning him. I was hoping you would help, but I see you are done washing. It would mean a lot if you would help me. See, I have already changed to my best dress."

Rusty thought, *How can you tell which is your best dress, you have so many.*

Rusty removed his leggings and wearing only a breechcloth said, "You undress him and hand him to me." When she did, she had to push the boy to get him near the water. The boy fell, he grabbed her leg causing her to trip and slide down the bank into the stream. Her best dress got wet and covered with mud. Rusty laughed and took hold of the boy. Setting Sun went into the shallow water and began to wash off some of the mud. He made the boy use his hands to wash himself and when Rusty was satisfied, let go of him and called to Setting Sun. "Take a good hold of him. He is slippery." The boy got away from her and ran down the stream bed. Setting Sun ran down the near bank and Rusty crossed the stream and ran after the boy on the other side where the water was deep. There was a curve in the stream and as the boy went past it, Rusty heard a growl.

The boy was standing still. In front of him was a grizzly bear. It was eating on the body of an Indian squaw. That squaw was Little Blackbird. Rusty called to Setting Sun.

"Stop! Go back for my big rifle, there is a bear here!" He wanted to tell the boy to come back slowly, but there was no way. The boy would not know what the words meant. The bear had so far stayed on its food. Rusty slowly walked over and picked up the boy and backed up. As soon as he dared, he crossed the deep water and reached the other side. He kept walking and was far from the stream when Setting Sun and some braves with guns came. He was still holding the boy, who had a tight grip on Rusty's neck.

"Sorry I took so long. I found your rifle, but could not find where you had powder and rifle balls. I went for help." Three braves went after the bear and came right back.

"The bear is gone. What it was eating is gone too. This was not a bear to rush after. We will shoot him later. Rusty, how close did you come to him?" asked Running Antelope.

"Too close because of this boy! If I was here, the bear was where my sister is standing."

"You are looked over by a good spirit."

"Maybe freckles are lucky," said Setting Sun.

They returned to the lodge to find their parents eating and Burned Face waiting for Rusty.

Before any could speak, Setting Sun told about the girl, Little Blackbird, being eaten by the grizzly bear.

"Your son was lucky to have gone so close to the bear saving this crying boy," said Setting Sun.

"Little Blackbird killed Black Knife. Walks Fast sent young bucks to catch her. She might have been better off with the bear. She was given to them to do with her as they wished. But that is not what I came for. Rusty, it will be some time before you are needed at the council gathering. You don't have Black Knife to work on. My woman, Pigeon

Girl, and I would like you to come and have some coffee with sugar at our lodge."

"Coffee, with sugar, here? How? Yes, I will come. Let me finish dressing. Real coffee. Is the sugar white or brown sugar? May I bring my sister?"

"Setting Sun is welcome."

"May I go? Cloud Woman, will you watch Cry A Lot boy?"

"Yes, this one time, but not all this day. I, too, have things to say at the gathering, and we must dress this boy. Let me have the old dress you saved from when you were a little girl. It will fit him."

"Not the blue and white one with silver bells!"

"Yes, that one," demanded Cloud Woman.

"Yes, but only till I find a something else for him to wear. I want it back. If he soils it, I'll scalp him!"

Chapter 7

Pigeon Girl welcomed Rusty and Setting Sun and had them sit while she poured the hot coffee into tin cups taken from gold miners. She used a buffalo horn spoon to add a heaping amount of sugar.

"Where is the coffee from? There is no trading near here," asked Rusty.

"We are trading with the people on the wagons that pass. They are poor hunters or fearful of losing scalps. Fresh meat is better to trade than furs. I got this coffee and sugar and some white flour all for the back half of a small deer."

"I have been too busy. The last I heard was to stay away from the wagons as some are fools and shoot first at any Indian. How has that changed?"

"What we have learned, my friend, is they don't fear squaws. Pigeon Girl came with me. I was in a blanket so they could not be sure. I showed no gun, but had my short shotgun hidden by the blanket. Some braves stayed on a hill not far but where they could be seen. How is your coffee?"

"It is welcome. I slept poorly last night and it was a short night, as you know. It will be the same today and tonight.

"It looks like married life suits you?" asked Setting Sun of Burned Face.

"Yes, good friend and sister of my best friend. I want to thank you both for the fine stories you both told for me. The people are still talking about them."

"Let us plan a bear hunt for the next day," said Rusty.

"It had better be soon. That grizzly bear will have many guns after him," said Setting Sun.

"It would be a great honor if you braves would let me join you in the hunt."

Her directness put them on the spot...

"I hate to spoil this party, but we must not be thinking about hunting a grizzly bear. They are hard to kill. I don't think you two would be allowed to hunt one. I am in my sixteenth summer, Setting Sun is only at fourteen and you, my friend, are still thirteen. I have never known the elders to let anyone under sixteen hunt bear."

"What if we were to hunt deer and just happened to find a bear. We would have to shoot it!" said Setting Sun.

"Tall Elk would shoot me if I let a grizzly bite your head off," said Rusty. "I thank you for the coffee. It is time we must go."

At the lodge they learned the crying boy liked wearing the dress with silver bells. Adding a belt and headband made it look better. Cloud Woman told them she had found a person to watch the boy for the day and until night. But they must come and get him to sleep with them.

Rusty went straight to the gathering where drums were sounding and a big fire was blazing, even during the day. He was given a seat next to Tall Elk and not behind him where Setting Sun and Walking Dove stood or sat. Walks Fast let the older brave, Sly Fox, start. He spoke of his past exploits, the many scalps he took, and went on about what other great warriors had done. Finally he got to his point. He unrolled a skin. It was over a yard across and showed a drawing with stick figures of the battle. He had the dead Crow, the Cheyenne, and he pointed to how some Cheyenne were fighting side by side. On the edge he had rows of small lines that gave the number killed on each side. This showed what a total victory it was. Rusty could see details like his father surrounded by four Crow, then killing the one as one ran. There was even Burned Face shooting Black Knife in the leg. Sly Fox called for Rusty to stand. He pointed to some of the Cheyenne braves fighting in pairs and shooting Crows. He spoke on and on about how Rusty, just a boy of twelve summers, had given so much good advice. "He must have a spirit speaking to him." Rusty was put out that his age was off a year. Setting Sun was quick to note the mistake and whispered, "Did you sell a year that was not good?"

Sly Fox called Tall Elk to come and stand forward with his son, Dreams A Lot. He gave a package to Tall Elk and said, "This is to be held in the lodge of Tall Elk because both father and son have earned the right to keep it for the Cheyenne. This important pipe will be a reminder of their help in winning the battle. The Crow chief, Bent Wing, had this one of the four peace pipes from the great council that Broken Hand made when I was a young brave." He opened the package and gave Tall Elk a long highly decorated pipe of the kind that was a tomahawk and long stem pipe.

Covered by the noise of people clapping and talking, Setting Sun whispered to Rusty, "Just a pipe? They should have given you many Crow ponies. I have news about the squaw, Little Blackbird." Rusty was ready to get out of the spotlight. He moved back and Setting Sun followed him.

"The bear did not kill that girl. The trackers and hunters that Walks Fast sent after the bear tell that the signs show the girl fell by the stream and broke her ankle. She only went a short way, then sat and cut her throat. The bear just helped himself to her meat. They did not shoot the bear; it went far away. I tell you this because I see you feeling bad. Maybe you think that if you did not make Black Knife think you were going to blind him, the girl would not have died. My brother, none of that was your doing. Put it out of your head and enjoy this day of honor, even if you only got a pipe and not ponies and lost a year of age," her last words said with a smile at her joking about his age. He was thirteen, not twelve as Sly Fox had told all, and he was sensitive about his age.

How does this girl always know so much so soon? he thought. "Thank you for telling me and your wise words. Will they think I am rude if I go and get something to eat? All I had this morning was Burned Face's coffee."

"Wait, here, I will make your leave and join you." Rusty thought, *She must want something.*

"This is not the way to our lodge," he said.

"No, we must give Cloud Woman cooking time and I have to stop and get Cry A Lot. Don't worry, we don't have to watch him. I need to move him to a second lodge. He has worn out his staying at one in just a few hours. He is what I want to speak about."

"Wait. I never have heard of Cloud Woman needing time to prepare food. She always has some. And how do you do it? You know so much as soon as it happens in the whole village."

"Cloud Woman is making something special, I asked her to. How do I know so much and get things done? I have many friends of the young squaws and many young bucks with my favor. I get the bucks to do things for me and the girls will, too, and they are always around because of the bucks. Our father says it is like I am a minor chief! Did you know that Walks Fast had the body of Black Knife rolled in a blanket and tied on a captured Crow pony to be returned within a short distance of the Crow village?"

"So this is why you are in no hurry to take a man. You would lose much of your power. Did I thank you for giving me the news about Little Blackbird? I can't recall. If not, thank you. Yes, it was heavy on my mind. Can we eat now?"

They stopped for the boy, Cry A Lot. He was wearing the plain clothes of a little girl. Setting Sun was given her good dress wrapped in a cloth. She was told the boy didn't like wearing just a breechcloth, or nothing as a five-year-old Cheyenne might, but cried less when given the dress of a girl. It was plain they were glad to get rid of him. An older squaw at the lodge where he was left off reminded Setting Sun of a promised gift.

Cloud Woman had used white flour and her iron Dutch oven to make a meat pie with a brown crust of biscuits. The crust was sprinkled with sugar. This was so unlike the Cheyenne cooking, Rusty could not believe it was real. He asked Cloud Woman where she had learned to cook like this. The older squaw paused and said, "It is not polite to speak of the dead, but I know Setting Sun will not mind. Her father, Quinn, was our guest many times. He liked to cook. I learned by watching him. I don't cook that way in respect for Walking Dove and Tall Elk. They are not here for this meal. Eat, make meat on your bones." She poked Rusty's ribs, a thing she enjoyed doing since he was ticklish.

When they were done eating, Rusty reminded Setting Sun that they were required to return to the council fire since they were the son and daughter of a chief.

"So what can I do for you? A something that is big enough to need a fine meal like this as a bribe."

"Help me get rid of Cry A Lot. I have a plan. I want to give him away to one of the people on the wagon trains that pass. That is where he came from. I need your help to do that."

"I don't understand. Is it your right to give him away? If you may, then just have one of the bucks that like to do as you ask take him and put him in front of some wagons."

"Our father said the boy may be given to the people that pass on wagons, but there is a problem. This morning some Cheyenne were shot at by whites on a wagon. They went to trade, with no guns in sight and braves guarding them at a distance. Gray Wolf was there. He told that it looked like some white man fell and his rifle fired. That started the others to fire at our braves. No Cheyenne was hit but a pony was shot. The braves then shot one of the mules pulling a wagon and went away. Father and Chief Walks Fast say no one may go near the wagons."

"Then how can I help?"

"You have the clothes of a white man. If you wear them, with your braids under a hat, you could go to one of the wagon train scouts that rides ahead and talk to him. Ask if he will take the boy, or say that the boy will be left near the trail, if none shoot at you. If you agree, I will take the blame if we are caught."

"That is a good plan, but we should ask permission. I will go do that now. I, too, will be glad to be rid of the boy."

Before Rusty could ask about getting rid of the crying boy, he was told to sit and hear more speeches. The braves that had made their first kill or first coups were given the honor of speaking. Rusty found their bragging boring. It was a struggle for him to keep from dreaming of what he would have done if he had been a part of the raid. During a break in the speeches, Tall Elk told him he should plan on doing something for Sly Fox and Falling Beaver.

"Father, may I speak with you away from this group?"

"Is it a matter that will not wait till tonight?"

"No, Father, it can wait."

"Then it will wait. My ears are busy. It is my duty as a chief to hear these young braves talk. Many will not get a chance to brag for a year or more. Don't you know there are several who are trying to make your sister think better of them?" A long time later, Tall Elk spoke of how the fighting was not all at the camp of the Crow. He said it was time for Walking Dove to speak. She was brief.

"Three Crow came to our lodge. They may have been looking for our son to take for Black Knife to torture. The same Black Knife that our son did teach about torture. I shot

74

one with a pistol and one with a rifle. The one I shot with a pistol did not die. I now ask Tall Elk's first wife to tell you more about our shooting of Crow warriors."

Rusty could not believe his eyes. Cloud Woman stepped out front. Her dress was the finest he had ever seen. The patterns of bead were so intricate. *It must have taken years to make that dress*, he thought. Then she spoke, loud for all to hear. Tall Elk handed her the shotgun she used.

"I, like my lodge sister, was ready when the foolish Crow came to our lodge looking for our son or maybe the beautiful mother and daughter that live there. I do not mean this person; my beauty is only in what these hands make. She showed off the dress. I tied a dog inside so we knew when the foolish Crow came. "I used this old but faithful shotgun to make a hole in a foolish Crow as big as this." She made a circle on her belly. "A hole a bird could fly through and not have its wings get wet with Crow blood. Sometimes these old guns only flash in the powder pan, so I pulled both triggers. Both barrels fired. That is what made the hole so big. The pistol used to shoot a second Crow by Walking Dove did not kill him. It took me two days to give him a message to take with him to the next life that he should have stayed away from this lodge guarded by two Cheyenne women." Then she sat and Walking Dove spoke giving the details of his torture. Torture that was done, not just by Cloud Woman but by several members of her beading society. The details made Rusty worry he was going to lose the fine meal he had just eaten.

Walks Fast stood and said that was all the speeches for this night. "Make a bigger fire and let all that will, dance."

"Father, may I now speak to you?"

"Yes, my son, talk."

"My sister has come up with a good plan to give Cry A Lot back to his people."

"If it is her plan, why are you talking to me? Has the Setting Sun I know gone shy? I could not believe that."

"Her plan is for me to dress as a white man and take the boy to one of the wagon train's scouts and ask him to take the boy. Braves could be near by to protect me, not that I would need help with one white man."

"I think maybe you are only twelve. Twelve or thirteen, your head is too big for your age. A Cheyenne of your age does not speak so of fighting one adult white man. I have seen great fighters in some whites. I will think on this. I too would be rid of Cry A Lot. Maybe he could be used as bear bait." Tall Elk said with a slight laugh.

That night, Cry A Lot lived up to his name. He would fall asleep, wake and start to cry. For a while, Rusty could get him to stop by telling him stories, even if the boy could not know what was said. Later when he started again, Cloud Woman said one more time and she would feed the boy to the dogs! Rusty pleaded with Setting Sun to let the boy sleep with her. "Maybe a woman's touch would work?" he reminded her of his promised help in getting rid of the boy. All were pleased when he stopped crying when Setting Sun pulled the boy under her blanket and the boy went to sleep.

There was a scream in the night.

"My bed is full of pee!" yelled Setting Sun. "He peed on me! I am all wet!" She pushed the sleeping boy onto the dirt floor. Rusty started to laugh, followed by all in the lodge except Setting Sun. She announced that she was going to the stream to wash. "Rusty, it was you who said this boy should be in my bed. You take him to the stream after I return!"

"No," spoke Tall Elk. Setting Sun does not tell my son what to do. That is for the adults. Rusty, get up, take a gun and go make sure no bear is at the stream. You can wait there till Setting Sun is done bathing. We will bring the boy."

"I will go with my daughter and I will wash the boy," said Walking Dove.

"Rusty, whistle for a dog to go with you," suggested Cloud Woman.

"Rusty and Setting Sun, in the morning dress so that you can take this boy to the wagons. If not, I shall tie a rock to him and drop him in the stream before he is here another night," said Tall Elk.

Rusty woke before dawn to find that Tall Elk was gone. They were eating first meal when he returned. "There are braves looking for wagons. It is a full day's ride to the wagon trail. You leave soon. Take extra food and bedding rolls. Setting Sun, dress Cry A Lot so they will want to keep him, even if it takes clothes you want to keep, is that understood?"

Tall Elk saw that Rusty was done eating. "Son, come with me." Both Twisted Nose and Running Bear were on horses with some young braves. "Twisted Nose is in charge. He will see to my family's protection. Son, speak your plan."

"I will dress as a white man. We watch for the dust that is made by the wagons. They should have a man riding ahead as a scout. I will go to one; the boy should be near. I will make white man's talk and try to get him to take the boy. If he says yes, I will wave like this. Setting Sun, not a brave, will bring the boy. The white man doesn't know my sister and will think she is a harmless squaw." That remark got a laugh from the young braves. "I will carry a pistol under my shirt. If there is no white scout to find but there are wagons, we will leave the boy tied to a spear in the ground ahead of them. I will stay near to protect him till they take him. That is my plan."

"No," said Tall Elk. "My son will only go to the white man scout with many braves where the whites can see and fear them. If the boy is to be left, he will not be tied to a spear, but tied on a pony with its legs hobbled so it can't run." He looked at Rusty and said, "A pony that belongs to Setting Sun." Then he said with a laugh. "Watch out for when your sister hears your joke about 'they will think she is a harmless squaw,' and she will hear that from one of these bucks seeking to win her favor. Now go and get her and the boy. I ride ahead." Tall Elk had changed his mind and was going with them.

Soon Rusty, Setting Sun and the boy were riding, following the dust trail of the braves ahead of them. The boy was tied on a pony led by Rusty and rode between them. He was smiling for a change.

"If I had known I was giving up a pony, I would not have let the boy wear the blue and white dress."

They stopped to rest the horses and eat at times. It became easier to leave the boy on his pony and walk the horses, except when the boy had to relieve himself. There were no wagons in sight. A camp was made not far from the wagon tracks.

"Setting Sun, it will get cold tonight. Shall I put Cry A Lot to sleep with you?"

"I would rather sleep with a skunk. Let him be with you till he sleeps, then move him to his own blanket."

There were no problems that night. Rusty let the boy sleep with him and two times got him up to relieve himself. They were eating the day's first meal when a brave came riding up fast. It was Running Antelope. "Tall Elk, there are three white men with a Crow coming. They are making signs they come in peace. One is an army man. He is dressed like he is the top chief of all soldiers in all of their armies!"

Tall Elk, Twisted Nose and Running Bear met and talked. Running Bear would wait out of sight but close with many of the braves.

Soon there were riders approaching. One was a man carrying a white flag. Just as was reported, a Crow scout rode with a buckskin-clad mountain man and a white man, whom they would later learn was the Wagon Master, and in the fanciest military uniform any had seen was a tall man with black hair, who wore a large hat of polished black leather with gold braid and white feathers. He rode with an air of authority. His uniform was covered with gold braided rope, medals and ribbons.

The mountain man introduced himself as Old Josh White and started to speak, but was interrupted when the boy saw the man in the fancy uniform. There were screams of joy and the boy and man spoke fast in the language of the boy. The boy climbed up onto the man's horse.

"We came here to get this boy back. What is your price?" said Josh White, the mountain man.

"Who is he?" said Tall Elk, as he pointed to the man holding the boy.

"This is the boy's uncle, Count Taddeus Padewski from Poland. The boy is Joseph Taddeus Padewski, a prince. He was lost four weeks ago when Pawnee attacked their wagons. How did he come to be with the Cheyenne? What will you take for him?" Then he turned his horse so the wagon master could not see his hands and spoke in sign language, saying something like, 'this is a very rich man and he is willing to pay much.'

The Cheyenne looked at each other. Tall Elk spoke, speaking in Cheyenne.

"Does this uncle the Count speak English?"

"Yes, better than I do," joked Josh White.

To his surprise, Tall Elk turned to Rusty. "Tell the uncle how we came by the boy, Cry A Lot, and what you paid for him." Tall Elk saw a puzzled look on Rusty and said, "Yes, the truth."

Rusty said, "This boy was a captive of the Pawnee. I gave them a fine Bowie knife for him. We are here, far from our village, because we were bringing the boy to the white man's wagons to get him back to his people. The Cheyenne were doing this not for reward or to sell the boy."

"A knife? For a prince?" said the Count uncle. He took off a fine gold and silver sword and handed it to Rusty. Then said, "I have no knowledge of what a Bowie knife is worth. Please take this sword made by the finest sword smith in all of Europe. Is there anything else that I can give to show my appreciation?"

There was a pause till Setting Sun spoke. "Our village is running short of coffee, sugar and flour." Those words drew her a stern look from Tall Elk.

The Count said if a guide could be provided, he would see that a wagonload of these things would be delivered.

Twisted Nose spoke to the Crow who was shooting dagger looks at Rusty.

"We sent Black Knife back to his people. Did he get there?"

The only answer he got was a nod.

The Count rode away. The Cheyenne did the same.

"That begging was not what the daughter of a chief should have done," Tall Elk directed to Setting Sun who replied, "Yes, Father, I am sorry. It is just the boy peed on me and I let him have a dress I loved."

They returned to find the village was being visited by Mandans who had escorted the missionary, the Reverend Anthony J. Thomas, who asked for a meeting with the chiefs and elders to tell him where they would be building him a church, a school and his home.

Chief Walks Fast told the reverend they would meet with him in a few days.

Two days later, a pack train of three overloaded mules arrived led by the mountain man, Josh White. Josh White spoke, directing his words to Rusty.

"Boy! You are one hell of a horse trader. Your act of bringing the boy out of kindness has paid off in riches. These three packhorses are yours—goods, mules, packs and all.

Plus, I have these gifts." He reached into a saddlebag and took out some packages wrapped in newspapers. He started with two smaller ones. "These are for the two adult squaws of the lodge of Tall Elk." Then a larger package. "This is for the girl that gave him the fine dress," then he laughed, "the one he pissed on!" Next a larger package. "This is for the lad Rusty, he even knew that name. It is for saving him from a bear. The pack loads are for the brave in charge of the lodge of Rusty and the girl." He started to ride off, leaving the lines of the pack mules drop.

Tall Elk invited him to stay and eat. He said he would be pleased to. "I want to see what you think of the goods on these pack mules."

They opened the packs one at a time. The first was full of five-pound bags of coffee beans and sugar. There were ten bags of each. The next mule load was of bags of flour, more coffee, and some one-gallon wooden kegs. Later they would learn the kegs were of pickles and sauerkraut. The last load was a big bag of potatoes, a small bag of onions and six big salted hams.

Setting Sun was the first to open her gift. It was jewelry—a necklace of pearls with a large ruby in the center. Walking Dove and Cloud Woman each received a bracelet of silver and small emeralds. Rusty opened his package and found it was two items. The first one was a genuine Bowie knife. It was engraved with the name Jim Bowie and a date. With it was a note from the Count. The note said that the sword was given in haste and confusion and would Rusty please consider returning it for these gifts? The second part was a flat wooden box that when opened contained a fine set of highly engraved single shot dueling pistols.

Rusty explained to Tall Elk that he had to return the sword. Cloud Woman looked at the necklace that Setting Sun had and said, "He could pee on me many times for a gift like that."

Cloud Woman knew how to prepare a meal of ham, onions and potatoes. Rusty talked her into heating some of the sauerkraut. He opened the pickles and passed some around. None had ever eaten dill pickles, and funny faces were made as some were given back after one bite. When they were done eating, since it was a hot night, they went out of the lodge and sat around a fire. Josh White reached into his saddlebag and came up with a small jug. Tall Elk said, "You are my guest, we will share your jug. It is a small one. I have to tell you I am not for whiskey. It makes Indians crazy." They only had passed it around once. Tall Elk only took a sip. Rusty was hoping to try some. He remembered when his brother George had sneaked a bottle of rum away from a party his family had. George was sure no one would miss it. He didn't remember if he liked the rum. Rusty did recall how he laughed at the way it made Ted and George act. Josh White was drinking with the jug held high when the Reverend Thomas walked right up and took the jug and smashed it on the ground. "The devil's brew!" he yelled and walked away. Tall Elk had to restrain Josh White from shooting the Reverend. "That was my last jug till rendezvous. It's a thousand miles to get more to drink. I'll kill him!"

Setting Sun wanted the Reverend to get started with a school. Rusty knew she was eager to catch up with him in book learning. He was pleased with the idea and offered her help, but she was not a good student when he tried to teach her. Their tempers and personalities clashed again and again when he tried to correct her use of words and understanding numbers. There were too many incidents with the Reverend before any real lessons could get started no matter how hard Rusty and Setting Sun tried.

"This man of God," as Walks Fast called him to Tall Elk, "has to go! In one day, he had preached against having more than one wife. He chased small children for not wearing clothes. He ripped a blanket from a young brave and

82

a squaw and burned some scalps that he found near the meat drying racks. He is your family's doing. You get him gone!" said Walks Fast to Tall Elk.

Tall Elk asked his brother, Twisted Nose, for help. One night when the scouts they sent said a wagon train was near, the Reverend was tied and gagged, put on a horse with his bags and left with his horse hobbled so it could not run in the path of the wagons. Rusty woke to find he was the owner of a book on the works of Shakespeare and a Bible.

Setting Sun could not resist pointing out that it was her doing that got them the coffee, sugar and hams.

"How shall we share this food?" Rusty asked Walking Dove.

Wait till Tall Elk comes back from...," she paused to laugh, "delivering the God man Thomas to his new flock. I don't think the wagon train people will keep him more than two days' travel. He could end up converting the Blackfoot!"

Rusty was pleased when Tall Elk and Walking Dove began to make piles of the foodstuff. Tall Elk named what was to go where. "A bag of coffee and sugar to...Cloud Woman's beading society."

Rusty quickly said, "Burned Face, yes."

"Walks Fast, Twisted Nose, Red Hatchet and White Hawk. How many is that?"

"Six," said Rusty.

"Stop, we will keep the next four to use when having visitors here," said Walking Dove.

"This bag of sugar is not to use. It is mine for my ponies," said Tall Elk.

"I'll give a whole ham to Walks Fast. And throw a feast for as many as we can feed with the rest."

"Maybe a ham and some potatoes and such should be set aside for an emergency," said Cloud Woman, who then said they should keep the wooden racks of the pack mules. "They could be good for hunters returning with much meat. When moving, I have beaded things that if on the packs would get less dust than on a travois."

"Mother Cloud Woman, I would have the two Fat Bellies, Sly Fox and Falling Beaver, here for a meal and listen to them talk. We could use some of this food."

"I would be pleased to do that. Is there any here that would join Rusty...us...in hearing them talk for a while?" she said with a chuckle.

At first no one spoke. Then Tall Elk did. "My son has remembered his duties, I will be here to greet them. Setting Sun, you will be here too. You will think to tell a young brave or two that I have said they may come here for that meal with you..., if they stay for the...short speeches of the Fat Bellies." Walking Dove used her hand to hide a laugh at 'short speeches.'

"I will make that meal and even stay awake for their talk," said Cloud Woman.

Setting Sun was putting on her new necklace. She didn't get the hook right and it dropped off. Cloud Woman put her hand on it and said, "I could sew this onto the top of a dress, then it would not fall off."

"Yes, thank you." Setting Sun began to choose which dress to use.

"Son, take this to the village crier and have him invite Sly Fox and Falling Beaver to our lodge for an evening meal. And you as but a boy should not be calling them 'Fat Bellies.' That is a name adults use to tease them." He gave Rusty a small piece of hide. Inside were two rifle bullets.

Cloud Woman had started to boil water in a big iron pot she had borrowed and began to cut potatoes into quarters when Rusty put his hand on her knife arm.

"Let me help. For a boiled dinner we always peeled the potatoes." He started to peel some. She took his knife from him.

Cloud Woman spoke to Setting Sun. "Go get more wood for the fire."

"But we have lots of wood."

"I said get more wood, now!"

Setting Sun knew when Cloud Woman meant something was not to be questioned and left.

Cloud Woman turned to Rusty. "So this little boy would tell me how to cook?" The next thing Rusty knew, he was picked up, dumped on his belly, and Cloud Woman was tickling him till he was giggling like a child and tears came to his eyes. "Now go! Tell your sister I do have plenty of wood. She is to find the braves she is bringing. I want to know how many? Tell me how many, then stay away till I call."

The dinner went better than planned. Setting Sun invited two young braves that were not the ones Rusty knew or expected. They were Spotted Deer and White Bear. They sat politely and ate, then listened to the two older braves talk. To their surprise, the older braves spoke a lot about the food, how good it was for Tall Elk to have these squaws and a brave son and beautiful daughter. They left telling Tall Elk he should have his son visit them to learn the old ways.

"Why were not Running Antelope or Gray Wolf or any of your regular braves here instead of these you never even talk to?"

"The word was you would know how to get the Fat Bellies to stop talking. I had the boys draw straws like in one of your stories. These two got the short straws. It is a fine joke on the others that this was not a long dinner, and they missed a fine but strange meal. Did you see that some of the potatoes had skin and some were naked?"

The village moved two times that fall. Rusty hunted many times using a bow and arrows to learn the old ways. He listened to the Fat Bellies about the habits of game and soon became a better trapper. All winter he was called on to read and tell stories. One very cold night, Rusty saw by the flickering light of the fire, Cloud Woman join Tall Elk and Walking Dove under their buffalo robes. Setting Sun then moved in with Rusty. He was rolling over to put his back to her when she took hold of his hand. She slid his hand under her dress and across her bare breast. He jerked it back and whispered, "What was that about?"

"Oh, just to make your heart work faster and keep me warm. Good night, little brother."

He whispered, "In my mind I see myself sitting in a chair. Stretched over my lap is a wicked girl. I am slapping her bare bottom. What girl do you think that is?"

"Brother, in your mind you are dreaming. I, however, am remembering spanking your white bottom till the red freckles did not show. Remembering is better than dreaming."

"Go to sleep! No, Setting Sun, put more wood on the fire, then go to sleep," said Tall Elk.

"Then we will have to bring in more wood before morning," she replied.

"That is the duty of the youngest squaw in a Cheyenne lodge. Go to sleep," said Walking Dove.

After putting wood on the fire, Setting Sun covered Rusty's mouth with one hand while the other tickled his ribs till he wiggled all over. Then she rolled her back to his back and very softly whispered, "Good night, little brother." Soon, the only sound was the snoring of Cloud Woman, a sound they were all used to.

That winter he went through most of the book by Shakespeare and even some stories from the Old Testament of the Bible.

Chapter 8

Rusty returned to the lodge when Tall Elk sent for him. The snow was almost gone and he had been racing ponies. He saw that Tall Elk had a thin blanket and was cutting it in half. Next he put some sugar in a small bag.

"My son, I hear you are learning to be a fast rider. I have traded for a very fast horse. This is for you to use riding him."

"That is very small!"

"Yes, but it will make you go faster. Let's go see if this new horse is worth the four ponies I traded for him."

"You talk as if you have not seen him?" questioned Rusty.

"I asked Twisted Nose to find the fastest horse. He visited many villages and had them race for him. That is why I had him look. No one knows horses like he does. This horse was taken from the white man's pony soldiers by the Sioux. It has marks that it was a Comanche pony. If he lets you ride him fast, you may give him a new name."

As they rode to where Tall Elk's part of the herd was, Rusty worked on a name. Twisted Nose was standing by a big, strong, black horse. It had a few white spots and a longer mane than most. At once, Rusty knew this horse should be named Samson, like the story he read in the Bible.

"This is a fine horse, but he has too much hair. We can cut some and he will have less weight to carry," said Tall Elk.

"No! Don't cut hair. See how he shakes his head. He is proud of his hair. He will get his speed and endurance from his hair. We shall name him Samson," said Rusty.

"What kind of name is that?" asked Twisted Nose.

"It is a name of a great warrior that won a battle by himself with only the jawbone of a mule as a weapon. He got his strength from his long hair. When an evil woman learned the secret of his hair, she cut it at night and he became weak and was killed."

"We will have the only Indian pony with a name like that. Samson it shall be. Rusty, make friends with Samson. Not at first, but soon let him smell sugar on your hand. Then if he lets you mount him, give him some, not much," said Tall Elk.

Rusty did as told. He took his time with the horse. It was bigger than his ponies and had a large chest. His patience and a little sugar worked. Before the day was half over, he was riding Samson. Tall Elk also rode Samson, and when Twisted Nose joined them, he and Tall Elk raced. Samson was fast but ran uncontrollably. If another horse was running with him, the rider had no control. Samson would not run behind another horse.

"It will take a long time to teach this horse to race if he will only run this way. Rusty, keep working with him. I will race him only in short races. It is in long races that he must learn to hold back to have a strong ending," said Tall Elk.

* * * * * *

With the threat of Black Knife over, Rusty was free to visit some of the other smaller villages of Cheyenne, even a Sioux village. Tall Elk and Rusty both raced Samson, winning all short races. At a Sioux village, Tall Elk let Rusty race in a longer race, being careful to not bet more than one pony. The Sioux were quick to see how to beat Samson in a long race, but they could not get Tall Elk to make a bigger wager. Rusty rode against six other ponies. Soon Twisted Nose told Tall Elk, "You will lose this race. See, they send pony after pony to challenge your horse for the lead. He is having to run hard against four; he will not set a steady pace." Twisted Nose was right. Rusty and Samson came in second.

Rusty said he was sorry. "We must have run too many races without his getting rest."

"No, on the ride to our lodge I will tell you what the Sioux learned and why we will not bet in long race with this horse. Be thankful we are returning with ten ponies we have won. You may pick out two as your own, and help your sister to pick one. When I was racing, what was it the young Sioux braves were speaking to you about?"

"They were asking if my sister was spoken for, and how many ponies it might take."

"What number did you give them?"

"I was bad. I told them only an old broken down mare and a mule. They laughed and knew I was not serious. If I had said what Setting Sun would think was the right number, no herd would be safe from braves stealing at night. Shall I tell her that?"

"Only when on a fast horse. Let us walk our horses and chew on pemmican. We are still most of a day's ride to our village."

* * * * * *

"Rusty! Wake up, you have a visitor," said Tall Elk.

"Who this early? It's still dark."

"It is our friend, Sam Hiller. He has a question for you."

Rusty turned, faced the outside of the lodge and dressed. Only the men were awake. There are no walls in a teepee lodge; privacy is only the facing away from others and their cooperation.

"Why so early, Father?" Rusty said as they walked towards the lodge of Chief Walks Fast. He could smell food cooking. The smell made him think of his mother's kitchen and the cooking of Isabelle, the cook-housekeeper of his white family. Inside the lodge, Berry Woman was using a huge skillet to fry ham and eggs.

"Ham and eggs! Where from?" Then he saw Sam Hiller.

"Hello, Rusty hair. A little bird said you were given some ham. Was it for your saving a Polish brat from a bear or his pissing on your sister in her bed? Tell me, did you give him lots to drink first?" That got a big laugh from Tall Elk and a chuckle from the others.

"I got eggs from an army cook. He packed them in loose powdered lime. He said they would keep a month that way. We shall see. That was only two weeks ago. Let us eat. I must leave soon and have a question for you."

The ham and eggs disappeared like a single snowflake hitting the ground. Tall Elk opened a blanket that was there and took out Rusty's Colt rifle and one of the leather arm guards.

It was Walks Fasts' lodge and as chief, he spoke first.

"Our friend, Sam Hiller, has made the army believe he is a great horse buyer. Because of a war in the east, the army wants to buy some of our horses and ponies. Sam will come here in a few days with the army to buy some. We are to not know who he is. That is one reason you are here, so you are told that. And he wants to ask about your rifle."

"Rusty, the Cheyenne horses will pay for new better rifles. Most of the ones here are single shot muzzle loaders. Of course that is what the war back east is being fought with. You have the only repeating rifle in this Colt. They are hard to find. I have seen few, I don't know why, so tell me about it, the good and the bad."

Rusty was so proud he had to stand and stick out his chest. "This rifle has six shots because it loads like a Colt pistol. A ramrod does not have to be pulled and used with each shot. The balls are put in with this little lever. It spits out from here and can burn your arm. I use this and then I can hold it like a true rifle. If not for this leather guard, I would have to hold it like this and could not shoot as well. It does not shoot as well as my long barrel Hawkins, but far better than a pistol. It must be cleaned after shooting many times or it will jam." While speaking, Rusty demonstrated what he was saying.

"This Colt costs a lot. There is a new rifle from Henry Company. It holds lots of bullets in a tube under the barrel, but it has a weak load. It too costs much. It will kill a man but is not a buffalo gun. And there is another called a Spencer that is a repeater. It loads from the stock. It has a more powerful load than the Henry, and the price is lower, but getting the bullets is more difficult than the Henry. I met a Pawnee that had a Henry. He said they call it Golden Boy gun because of the brass parts. I held it and like the feel better than this Colt. I won't be able to bring one of each and let the Cheyenne pick which I am to buy. The choice will be what I can get, but it is best to know how my friend, the Cheyenne, feel. Who here have used this Colt?"

"I am sad that I did not think to let others use it. Would my chiefs like me to return with powder and lead ball for them to fire this rifle?"

"No," said Walks Fast. "We will talk. You may go. Leave the rifle. Your father will give it back."

When Rusty left, it was decided to sell no more than four hundred horses, and then only for gold coin. After much discussion that had to end so Sam could leave, he was advised to buy rifles with the Colt at first choice then the Spencer and the more expensive Henry Golden Boy as a last choice. "The Colt uses loose powder and ball, like we have. The other repeating guns use special bullets that we may have a hard time getting. Yes, Sam, we know those kind will work better when it is raining. Time for you to go. May the good spirits be with you," said Walks Fast.

Rusty returned to find the women eating first meal. Cloud Woman spoke. "Sit and eat, tell what you were doing with the chiefs."

"Thank you. We were talking about rifles. I ate food there. Sam came with eggs. I had ham and eggs!" He started to sit away from where the rest were eating. Cloud Woman put meat and soup in a wooden bowl and gave it to him.

"When I say eat, you eat until I cannot feel these ribs," she said while a hand ran over his ribs, making him giggle in spite of his best efforts not to.

"Oh, Setting Sun, I know something you don't. Sam Hiller will be coming here with army men to buy horses. We are to act like we don't know him."

"How could I know that, since I am only worth an 'old broken down mare and a mule.'" Then she smiled and Rusty choked on a piece of meat till Walking Dove hit his back.

* * * * * *

In late spring, Rusty learned that some braves were going to meet with trappers at what was called a rendezvous. He asked Tall Elk what it was like, wondering if he should ask for permission to go.

"This may be last of these gatherings. The fur trade is about over. Years ago, I went to a rendezvous to trade beaver pelts for gunpowder. It was a wild place. The mountain men that lived all year trapping alone would meet with traders that would buy their furs and sell them supplies. Many times the pay was whiskey, and men got crazy in the head and lost a year's work. There were games, races and shooting with betting. There were also braves that got to drinking whiskey and would trade their squaws for more. It is not the Cheyenne way to tell our braves they may not go there to trade, but we are letting them know that this tribe has no room for any that bring back the white man's poison, whiskey. It would not be a safe place for you."

* * * * * *

A brave came riding fast calling that some soldiers were coming. "There is a man with a white flag and an army officer soldier coming in front." Sam Hiller called out in Cheyenne that they came in peace with rifles not ready to shoot. Riding with him was a Major that had only one arm. Both were covered with dust. The Major wore a uniform that had seen better days and in the east would have been replaced at once.

The white man Sam called that they were here to buy horses for the Union Army. He was met by Tall Elk and White Hawk who acted like they didn't know him. A brave rode out and led the rest of the soldiers and four civilian cowboy wranglers to the stream where they were told to stay till needed. Rusty, like many, came to see them wearing a blanket and looking more like a squaw than a brave. He heard it said that these soldiers were from the south and were let out of a prisoner-of-war camp by joining the Union Army of the west.

"Look them over good! These will be the soldiers that we have to fight if they come back to kill the Cheyenne," said Running Bear.

It was a warm day and Walks Fast held the dealing for horses in front of his lodge in the sun. He offered no water to the two officers and Sam. The Major didn't know that Sam had informed Walks Fast that the army was willing to pay fifty dollars a head for horses. There were the usual polite words except for Walks Fast reminding the Major that the treaty said the army was to keep white men out of Cheyenne lands, and that included those that looked for the yellow metal.

Sam spoke of the great war to save the country and that the army would pay thirty-five dollars a horse. Tall Elk was chosen to bargain.

"We have sold many to the army before for fifty-five dollars. Now that the army is more in need of good horses, the price is sixty—no less."

Sam spoke to the Major and went to forty, then forty-five.

Tall Elk spoke that if these men came all this way, he might sell them one hundred for only fifty-five. Sam and the Major spoke in whispers.

"The U.S. Army will pay fifty-five for the first two hundred. If the Cheyenne will sell three hundred more for only fifty dollars each."

This was a hundred horses more than was planned. It would take a deal of talking, since the tribe as a whole owned none. All were owned by braves, many that counted the number of horses as their standing in the tribe. The braves that owned the most horses also were braves that already had rifles. Tall Elk had to ask the Major and Sam for more time. It would be necessary to get them away from the village to talk over selling one hundred more horses.

"Let us have the soldiers inspect our horses, and stay for a feast of buffalo. There is a small herd nearby. We invite the soldiers to join us in killing some. The Major was delighted and knew his men would be as well. He assigned the civilian cowboys to inspect the horses, and let his men follow some braves to ride and shoot a few buffalo. Rusty was disappointed when he was told to stay in the lodge. Setting Sun had not been told, so she talked Rusty out of his Hawkins rifle and rode with the braves over their protests. She rode a fast pony and was one of the first to kill a large calf. The soldiers that watched her cheered her kill. She heard a soldier say that if there was war with these Indians, he would take her for himself. She rode close to him and waved her long knife under his nose saying in English, "I would cut your heart out, fool."

It took a while to get the right to sell one hundred more horses. An elder went to Rusty and asked if he could make numbers on paper and help Walks Fast with knowing if the pay given was as it should be. Sam had written it down before what the pay for four hundred horses at fifty dollars would be. Now it was different and Sam could not help them. He was never fully trusted when it came to money or gold. Even before the trading, Sam had told the army that these Cheyenne would only sell for solid gold or silver coins, no paper money. He had a chest. The soldiers and cowboys were helped separating the horses to be sold. A place for the soldiers to camp was set aside. There were guards by both army and Cheyenne.

Rusty, stuck in the lodge, began to read again the book by Shakespeare. The only story in it he had not read was *Romeo and Juliet*. The first few pages had not interested him as much as *Hamlet* and other stories of kings. Then when he read it a second time, he began to think of how he could retell it. The two feuding families could be different Indian tribes. The brave from one and the girl from the other. *This is a story for Setting Sun's friends to enjoy,* he thought. Rusty was alone in the lodge, hoping somebody would come and tell him when the soldiers would leave. Setting Sun came, she was angry.

"No one said I could not hunt! Or shoot! I am as good as many of the braves. It is so unfair."

When she calmed down, he learned that the soldiers were to spend the night, and there was to be a feast of fresh buffalo meat. She had shot a buffalo, but the elder braves didn't think she should have.

"Father gave in to those old men, and I am to stay here till the soldiers are gone, just because someone saw the way the soldiers looked at me!"

"I am sorry sister. I can help if you will let me."

"How can you help? You are stuck here, too."

"There is a story in this book I have been saving to read for you and your friends, the young girls, that is. It is a love story. I am sure you and your friends would like it. Can you get three or four to come here and I shall read it while the feast is with the soldiers. Just see that I get fed."

"I am told not to leave this lodge. How can I get them here?"

"I will find a person. Who of the girls is the nearest to here? Wait, I hear voices." Rusty saw a young girl walking to get water. Her name was Cricket. She was one year younger than Rusty and he had seen her give him looks and smiles when swimming.

"Wait, Cricket, come here! Would you help me? Go and find Winter Rose or Voice Like A Man and send them here, now. Yes, you can get your water first. What do I want?" He looked at Setting Sun for help, who put her head out of the lodge and spoke to the girl in whispers.

"She will get you a group for your story telling. I hope it is good story. I had to let her come, too."

Walking Dove came and told Setting Sun that it might be unfair for her to be made to stay in the lodge, but it was for her own and the tribe's good. "Don't you know you got some soldiers excited? You riding with your legs showing and shooting. Braves will have to watch carefully that no foolish soldiers try to come after you tonight. Some soldiers think Indian women are just for the taking. Cloud Woman will bring you food." She turned to Rusty. "You must stay here. Could you find a story in your book to read to your sister? If you will, it would please me."

Rusty had trouble keeping a straight face as he said, "Yes, to please you and the harmony of this family, I will somehow find a story for my sister, even if I have to tie her down to get her to hear it."

As the sun went down, young girls began to climb through the door flap. First there were four, then eight, then six more came. Rusty said there were too many. The heat would kill him. He had to have a fire for light to read.

Only a few heard him start to read, as many were talking. He started again and again. Then he stopped trying to read and told that this was a love story, and they got still and listened. He almost lost his temper when he read the lips of a girl asking Setting Sun how could a shy virgin like her brother tell of love? Rusty was fourteen and dreamed about girls at night.

"This is a story of a beautiful Cheyenne maiden and the boy she loved and wanted to marry. They met at the outside of a trading post. She was a Cheyenne and the handsome brave was a Blackfoot. And her father, a chief who was at war with the Blackfoot, and the Blackfoot clan of the brave had lost many braves to battle with the Cheyenne of her tribe. But she saw him and fell in love as soon as their eyes met." It dawned on Rusty that there was no sound coming from his audience. As he continued, Tall Elk put in his head and left. Soon Walking Dove did the same. Rusty told the story jumping from words by Shakespeare to his telling of what was happening in terms of Indian behavior. He did stick to the facts about the poison and the double suicide, the one dying with a dagger. He acted out that part using Setting Sun's Arkansas toothpick and stuck himself, only hitting the point into a piece of wood he had under his shirt the whole time as he fell and hammed it up. He saw tears in the eyes of some girls. "Again, again! Tell it again," he heard. "I can't. I'm too hot. Maybe another time." He did not see Setting Sun look to Winter Rose who came to Rusty and took off his shirt.

"Now we don't have to have the dagger. Please tell it again for me."

A girl took a stick and propped the door flap open and another made the flap at the top of the tepee more open.

Setting Sun lit a tallow lamp made from a buffalo horn and kicked the fire apart. Cricket held the lamp near Rusty. He started to tell the story over and soon had a problem. He had forgotten the Indian names he had given to Romeo and Juliet. He paused, and then explained that for the Cheyenne it was not polite to speak of the dead, and this boy and girl were dead so he would not use their names. He would call them Romeo and Juliet. He finished telling the story without falling when stabbing himself. Lacking a piece of wood, he faked stabbing by sticking the blade under his armpit. He told it a third time mostly for the crowd of girls and adult squaws that were sitting outside listening.

Setting Sun stood and said, "That is all. My brother is done for the night. All please to go." Then she watched laughing as the girl Cricket thanked Rusty and paused to hug and kiss him. That made some of the other younger girls feel they could do the same. Rusty pushed them away as best he could while blushing. Winter Rose and Voice Like A Man stayed, making it a problem for Rusty to deal with his embarrassment of the bulge that was pushing at his breechcloth. He sat and held his book of Shakespeare on his lap.

"Rusty, you have done too fine a job as a story teller. You know that you will have to read that story to the whole village, except the braves, and there are some of them that might want to hear it."

Tall Elk came into the lodge. Winter Rose started to leave. "Stay, I am only here for a minute. I came to tell my son and daughter how sad I was about their having to stay here for the evening. But I don't think I'll say that." He looked at the visiting girls. "Son, when these young squaws leave, carry your rifle and walk them to their lodges. Then return here."

After answering their questions about this Shakespeare, like, where could Rusty get his new books, and was this a real story, and in what land, Winter Rose teased Rusty, asking Setting Sun if she and Voice Like A Man had to hug and kiss her brother like the youngest girls before they could leave. Rusty was fully armed with rifle, tomahawk and Bowie knife.

The lodge of Voice Like A Man was near. At the lodge, she turned and kissed Rusty, a good solid kiss that made him blush. "That is for the story. I shall dream of it for many nights. Thank you."

Winter Rose lived with her uncle, White Hawk. It was on the far side of the village. Rusty saw White Hawk speaking with one of the cowboys that had come to take the horses. When they reached her lodge, Rusty asked if she would be safe all alone. "Maybe I should stay till White Hawk returns, or I could stay until you have a big fire so soldiers will think many people live here." Winter Rose started to go in, holding the door flap open, she pointed to Rusty. "See the many weapons hanging. You helped me learn to use some. I will be safe, thanks." He turned to leave. "Stop! Boys are so easy to tease. Here, storyteller, your reward." Then she kissed and hugged him, holding him and saying, "I will not let go till you blush!" A second kiss did that. Rusty walked the wrong way going back to their lodge, till someone asked, "Rusty, are you lost?"

Chapter 9

It was late morning before the soldiers left with the horses. Rusty went for a walk and was stopped by Berry Woman, wife of Chief Walks Fast, who asked when he would be reading his love story to the older squaws? During the next few days he would read *Romeo and Juliet* many times, till he was sick of it. He hid the book and tried to use that as an excuse for not telling it.

At evening meal, Walking Dove said how pleased she was with having a great storyteller for a son. Tall Elk spoke. "Story-telling is good for long nights but will not feed a lodge."

"Ask my storytelling brother what reward he got from a certain girl he is crazy about."

Rusty excused himself to go and practice with his sling. He was soon joined by ten- and eleven-year-old boys that wanted him to teach them the sling. *I taught Setting Sun and Winter Rose the sling, I can teach these boys,* thought Rusty. "This is now Rusty's school. You six are my first students. I will make all of you masters at killing with a sling. You will have to always be here for practice-school, and as a return gift for my time, you will each day bring me one armload of firewood. I will tell you where to take the wood when we are done. One boy said no, the rest stayed. He demonstrated the sling, using his old coffee pot lid as a target. It made a loud ring when hit. He had each boy try it five times taking turns; his encouragement worked. For his first lessons he had them close to the target. When he saw they were tired, he reminded them to bring the firewood each lesson. "Maybe with this school I will be a better teacher than I have been with Setting Sun.

"Can my brother take lessons, too?" asked a boy named Jumping Dog.

"Yes," said Rusty, "but that will make six. No more students for this class. Only when you are masters with the sling will I start a second class. Later, Cloud Woman helped him make six new slings of deer hide from an old dress of Setting Sun's. Having the class give him something else to do besides storytelling, with which he was getting bored. His students were also delivering firewood to his lodge. When there was too much at his lodge, he had them take wood to the elders, starting with Chief Walks Fast, Iron Hand, Red Hatchet the Shaman, White Weasel the Medicine Man, and the lodge where the older squaws did beading. Soon his students were gathering wood for many of the tribe. In only ten lessons he started his second class. This time he took ten students.

"Rusty, you must make an end to this sling school you do. It is good, but the elders have said it is not the Cheyenne way. Boys should learn from their older brothers and cousins and fathers. It was only allowed because this sling of yours is new. Now it is not, and the telling how to do a hunting skill for pay is not our way," said Tall Elk one morning at first meal.

* * * * * *

Sam Hiller returned and left with money from the sale of horses. Two braves went with him. They would dress as his slaves. Both were armed. One brave was loaned one of the dueling pistols the Polish Count had given Rusty. Sam's plan was to go to Fort Deerborn, what is now Chicago. There, he would claim to be arming his stagecoach company. His trip took a month going by horse, stagecoach and riverboat, then they had to buy more horses. It was with difficulty that he explained to the braves with him that it was safe for him to leave the money at a bank. They stayed in a hotel, and ate, slept and watched out the windows the many people. He was two weeks buying the rifles he wanted. In the end, he was bribing salesmen at hardware stores and gun jobbers. One night when Sam was running out of places to buy the newer rifles, he was the winner in a poker game. After the game, a man that had lost heavily approached Sam in the hall.

"I lost more than I should. Give me back fifty dollars of what I lost and I'll save your life."

The man looked serious, so Sam agreed.

"You are being watched by the Pinkertons, the detectives. They think you are buying guns for the rebels. The only reason you have not been arrested and turned over to the military is they are waiting for you to make contact with southern sympathizers. Selling guns to the south is a hanging offense, after a fast army trial."

That night he had one of the braves start a barn fire to distract the police and let them slip away with what guns they had.

They left in July, and once across the Mississippi River, they traveled only by horse going far north to go around problem areas. It was known that the village would be moving. A system of signs were left at key points to direct them. Scouts were getting nervous, out looking for his return day after day. When he did return, it was at the end of August.

One of the braves brought a calendar from a hotel room that had many drawings by Currier and Ives of Indian chiefs and famous battles. Rusty was asked to read what was said under the prints. He was given the pages with numbers and now had a calendar.

"Now I'll know when my birthday is," he told Setting Sun. "Next month I shall be fifteen."

Sam had returned with the rifles and half of the money from the sale of the horses that he took. The braves had many tales about their travel. He could not get as many Colt rifles as he wanted; he was told it was the war and production was slow as that gun did not sell very well. He explained that the Spencer carbines were impossible to find as individual soldiers were having their families buy them and he had only a few. Only the Henry rifles were available in any number. He would have gotten more but had to leave before his order came from the factory in New England. He was pleased to show that he had purchased two large cases of bullets for the Henry and Spencer rifles. He had two hundred cartridges for each of those forty rifles he was able to buy. When Sam got confused changing from horses to money to rifles, he had Rusty take pencil and paper and help him come up with a fair count. Some braves got money back for their horses, others told Sam to hold it till he could get more rifles. He only had ten Colt rifles. Rusty was asked to show the braves how to load and use them.

* * * * * *

"Setting Sun, wake up."

"What for? It is still dark."

"Hunting. You say you want to hunt. Now I am asking if you want to go and try to shoot an elk with your brother."

"Yes, who is going?" she asked, as Rusty turned and faced the fire while she dressed. She was slow and he turned too soon. She smiled as he quickly turned back around.

"Sorry," he said. It was at times like this that it was hard to think of her as only a sister. He saw that now her hips were wider and her breasts had grown from the size of plums to peaches.

"It is all right, we are sister and brother. I asked who is going, not just us?"

"I confess my friends left last night to sleep near where the elk have been seen. I was telling a story and could not go.

This morning Gray Wolf came back for a different rifle. His broke. I was out for a walk and met him. He says the elk are even closer to the village. They did not have to sleep on the ground. If you like you can use my Hawkins. I'll use my Colt. Your rifle is too small for elk."

"Thank you, but I want to prove that my rifle will kill an elk. I had a long talk about it with the best hunters. If I shoot at the head or the right place in the neck, my rifle will bring down an elk. Let us go."

They rode ponies. Rusty brought a packhorse with one of the wooden cross pack carriers that came with the Polish Count's gifts. The sun was up but low in the sky when Rusty said, "We tie our ponies here and hunt on foot. There is a meadow with a spring we should watch, it is over this next hill. Is your rifle loaded?"

"You always keep asking me that! Yes, it is and I have a cap on it, see?"

He was starting to answer her when he froze and pointed.

"Stand still. Some elk are coming. Other hunters must have moved them. We should only shoot one. I will let you shoot first."

"Don't shoot my elk! I have a something to prove."

"Shut up, foolish girl! I will not shoot if your elk drops, but a Cheyenne hunter does not let a wounded elk run off."

"Now who is talking too much?" she said, as she braced her rifle on a tree and fired.

Rusty could not see the smoke. He saw the closest elk stumble then rise. He aimed where the neck joins the body and fired. They could hear it drop. Setting Sun began to run towards the elk.

"Stop! Load your rifle first. He was pulling out the ramrod and starting to load his when she gave him her rifle and ran. "Here, you load it!"

He loaded his while walking and left hers by a tree. "I can't load yours. My rifle balls are too big. You should know that."

She was looking down on a large elk. It was dead. She tested by touching an open eye. "See, you did not have to shoot! My hit is right here."

A tiny spot of blood was under the ear of the elk. A second larger spot was below that. Rusty looked at them. When moving the head, blood shot out of the bullet hole she had made.

"Yes, sister, you killed this elk. I just reminded him that he was dead. Here, take this." He gave her his rifle. "I will go for the packhorse. The trees are not so thick. I believe I can get it here. While I am gone, what should you do, sister hunter?"

"I shall start to clean this fine elk, foolish boy."

"Wrong. First get your rifle and load it! How many times must I tell you!"

Before he could speak, she said, using his voice, "It is but a heavy club if not loaded with powder and ball."

While Rusty went for the packhorse, Setting Sun first began to cut open the elk's belly. Then she remembered her rifle left by a tree. She was loading it where she left it when she saw that her elk was moving.

"What?" she said out loud. Rusty came up leading the packhorse. "Something is stealing my elk! See, it has moved."

"Wait here." He walked slowly then stopped. She was right behind him.

"Did you hear that?"

"No, hear what?"

"Don't speak," Rusty warned as he removed his Colt rifle from the special scabbard Cloud Woman had made for him. The Colt was on the packhorse that began to jump and snort in fear.

"There is a bear at your elk. Stay here. Is your rifle loaded yet?"

"Yes, and so is yours, but the bear has it. I have my pistol as well." She took out her Colt pistol from inside her jacket and put it in her belt.

Rusty held his Colt rifle ready and walked to where they had last seen the elk. A giant seven-foot tall grizzly bear stood on its back feet. Then it backed off.

"We might be able to scare it. Don't shoot yet, I don't want a wounded grizzly running around where others are hunting. Stay ready to shoot one time, then climb a tree. I'm going to slowly walk over and see if I can get my Hawkins."

Rusty got almost to his Hawkins rifle when the bear charged. With no other choice, he backed up holding his Colt six-shot rifle ready to fire. He knew that at times a bear would make a false charge. That is what he hoped for. The grizzly bear stopped at the dead elk, too close for Rusty to get the more powerful Hawkins rifle. Setting Sun, with her small caliber rifle and pistol, walked to be at Rusty's side.

"Get back," he yelled. Seeing the two of them near his meat, the bear charged. Rusty fired three shots at the bear's head. The bear slowed down, shook its head and came at him. He then shot at the near shoulder of the bear. The last shot of the .44 Colt did damage. The bear fell, but only for a second, then it was up, nursing one front leg. Setting Sun distracted the bear by shooting at his face with the pistol. This made the bear stop and look, trying to decide who to go after. It stood on its back legs, giving Setting Sun the chance to throw her rifle to Rusty. At about ten feet, he aimed at the center of the bear's neck, just under its jaw and fired. Then he ran around a tree and yelled for Sun to find a tree.

"Our guns are empty, climb!" he yelled.

"What for, looking for squaw wood? This bear is dead. See?"

Setting Sun was poking the bear with her foot. Rusty came closer, and immediately ran and picked up his Hawkins rifle.

He looked at Setting Sun. She seemed so calm. His heart was racing. He wondered if she knew what danger they had been in.

Braves began coming to them from both sides.

"I heard a lot of shooting," said Burned Face.

"Who shot the bear?" asked Twisted Nose when he came with a ready rifle.

"We both did," said Setting Sun. "It was trying to steal the elk I shot."

Gray Wolf came holding Rusty's packhorse. "I caught this horse running away from here."

"Looks like we need a second packhorse just for this bear," said Rusty.

Burned Face, who liked to tease, spoke, pointing at Setting Sun. "Good thing we have a squaw to cut up and skin all this game." He looked for a reply from her, only to see her sit on the ground and begin to load her pistol. She looked at Rusty and said, "Have you reloaded your Colt rifle? You know it is but a heavy club without powder and ball. Oh, I can't wait to see Sam Hiller and have him tell again what he said about meeting a grizzly bear with only this rifle."

Rusty and Setting Sun were glad for the help with getting the bear and elk back to the village. With all their shooting, they did not hear as four more elk were shot before the killing was called to a halt. When the bear was skinned, they learned that Rusty's three hits on the bear's head had glanced off bone, doing no damage. Of the shoulder hits, one had hit into the ball socket stopping the use of that leg. None of the shots would have killed the bear. Three small holes were there from Setting Sun's pistol, one in the skin on the back of the neck, one through the open mouth that only hit skin, and one in the big meat of the back. It was pointed out to Rusty that his shot that broke the bear's neck was just in the right spot. "If this shot was even a finger off, you two would be bear food," said a serious Tall Elk. Cloud Woman showed how to cut out the bear claws to make either a necklace or decorations. Setting Sun said they must go to Rusty. She would put a tooth from the bear and the elk in her good luck bag. That day there was feast on elk meat, and around a fire, hunters told of their kills. All waited for Rusty to tell about the bear. When called to speak, he sat.

"My manly-woman sister should tell. You hear me speak too many times."

"But you killed the bear!" said Burned Face.

"Only because my sister knew to have her rifle loaded and that I was in a better place to make a killing shot, or she would have shot it. Let her tell. That is all I will say. And I have to save my words for some that want a story for just them."

He heard Berry Woman tell an older squaw that Rusty has love stories and young girls are waiting to hear them.

* * * * * *

"Rusty, go to your lodge, there are blue coat soldiers coming," said Tall Elk.

Standing near the lodge, Rusty learned that there were only forty horse soldiers. They had three wagons, one with supplies and two long ones of a type not seen before. The first four that rode up were with a man in a civilian suit. They had a white flag, and the soldiers did not have their rifles at a ready carry. Coming from near the wagons, after it was seen that they would be greeted peacefully, were two Crow army scouts. Each wore a soldier's cap and half an army jacket. Rusty dressed as a squaw and joined the many that were watching. When the speaking was to be done at the edge of the village and not while sitting with smoking, he grew suspicious. Those that understood English repeated what was said. During the talking, ten of the soldiers came to join those speaking with the chiefs. The message seemed to be that there was a peace meeting a day's ride to the south. The Cheyenne were being asked to send their chiefs, up to twenty were to come under the protection of the soldiers. The chiefs were not happy with this request and were asking for more details. Rusty moved so he could read the lips of an officer that was not with the main four but looked to be in charge of the others. Rusty learned that this was a trap. The wagons were to carry the chiefs away. They would not be coming back. He heard something about that the army had few soldiers because of the war, and to keep from fighting Indians, they were rounding up the Indian chiefs to send to a place called Florida. Rusty ran to Tall Elk. He yelled in Cheyenne, "This is a trap. These soldiers are lying. Don't go!" But he was turned away. He saw Red Hatchet. He remembered his telling Red Hatchet about his gifts to know what was said when he should not know. He yelled again and got the attention of Walks Fast and Red Hatchet.

"Your son, Dreams A Lot...Rusty is going mad, but I will hear him."

Rusty saw that the Crow seemed to be aware of Rusty. He read the lips of one that said to go and warn the soldiers at the wagon. Rusty called to White Hawk, "Don't let these Crow leave, they mean harm!"

Quickly a word from White Hawk and many braves began to surround the officers talking with the chiefs. The Crow were looking at many rifles and braves with bows and arrows. Rusty told Walks Fast that it was a trap, a trick, and they should take the guns from these men that lie.

"How does a boy know what is in the minds and hearts of these men that say they come in peace? And who gave a boy the right to tell chiefs what to do?" said Walks Fast.

Rusty had no choice. It was his secret or the life of is father, Tall Elk.

"I can read what men say by looking at them and seeing the words on their lips! Ask Red Hatchet. I told him I could long ago. Sorry I act too big for my station, only this is an emergency. Have a brave look in those back two wagons. There are chains to hold many Indians. Would they be peaceful if you are to go with them in chains?"

Walks Fast sent a brave to look, and he went back to the officers. "Tell me again you came in peace. Tell me the names of the chiefs of other tribes that are at this meeting I know nothing about?"

The brave sent to look in the wagons was turned away. He cried that out, and soon more Cheyenne with rifles were around the wagons. There were four braves for each of the nervous soldiers. A brave dared to climb in the back of a wagon. He saw wooden benches with leg iron chains on the floor. He called that out and a senior brave ran with the news to Walks Fast, who cried a few loud words and rifles and arrows were pointed at all the soldiers. None dared to move.

He spoke to the officer in charge. "Save the lives of you and your men. Tell them to put on the ground all guns and speak truthful to the Cheyenne." There was no immediate action. He spoke and the Crow scouts were shot full of arrows as a warning. He spoke again. "Where were you to steal us to with these wagons? Was it to kill us, or take us away?"

The officer, a Major, looked around and said, "If we disarm, will we be massacred?"

"No! We are not like the soldiers that fight women and children, shooting them in their sleep. You must first speak, not with a forked tongue. I will only ask one more time. Where were you planning to take us?"

The Major was sweating when he said, "We only want peace. The chiefs would be held away from their people till the army is done fighting in the east and we can man the forts to protect white people."

While this was being said, more braves moved closer and any soldier that made a move to reach for a rifle was warned and backed off. There were many southern voices saying things about being better off in a prisoner of war camp than scalped because of poor officers.

"Where is this Florida place?" asked Walks Fast.

The Major was stunned. That was a military secret. How could they know? It was a plan to remove many chiefs, principally the war chiefs, the Cheyenne were the test of this plan.

"Florida is far to the east and south."

"Is there not a war of north white men against south white men, a war with fighting in that south?" asked Walks Fast.

"The chiefs would be held in forts in the east till the war is over and they can be moved to Florida." As soon as he said that, he realized his mistake. Walks Fast saw it.

"You lied when you said, 'Keep chiefs only till war was over.' Who is next in charge under you?"

When the Major did not answer, Rusty spoke. "It would be him." He pointed to a Captain.

Walks Fast spoke to the Captain. "If your men put down their guns and walk, no horses, no wagons, we will let all go, but not him!" The Captain was unsure of himself. The Major, a brave man, told him to do as the chief told.

"Captain, take charge of A company, 3rd cavalry. See that my command returns as a unit, not a defeated mob."

The Captain gave an order for all guns and weapons to be put down. Then he spoke. "What are we to do, walk away? What about food and a ride for our men that get sick?"

"You may take two horses and what food ten men can carry. My braves will stay near and watch you. It is not a one-moon walk to where there is a fort. If your men get weak from hunger, my braves will shoot a buffalo and leave it for you. You may take a knife for that. Now go, never come back to the Cheyenne with lies!"

The soldiers complained, but once they saw that no shots were fired at them, they walked faster. Ten soldiers stripped the supply wagon of what they could carry, spreading their load among others once they started walking. But any could see that would not feed them for long.

There were two black soldiers. One was young. Rusty spoke to him. "Are you a freed slave? Would you like to stay here and join the Cheyenne? You would be treated better here."

"No, sir, thank you. I gets paid. Indians don't gets paid, do they?"

"We don't need money," said Rusty as the boy ran to catch up with the others. A brave found a book in the supply wagon and gave it to another saying, "Give this to the son of Tall Elk."

Rusty wanted to speak to the chiefs about his lip reading. Could they not tell all about it? But he could not get near them. The Major that lied was being stripped of his uniform. Rusty didn't see Walks Fast tell a squaw to not tear the uniform.

"Some day I may have a need for it. Maybe Rusty will wear it."

"It is too big," said a squaw.

"That can be fixed," said another as she rolled up the uniform.

The Major was tied and pulled by a rope towards the center of the village. Walks Fast was leading him, going slow so many squaws could hit the man. Rusty saw his father, Tall Elk, was riding with Walks Fast. He saw and ran to Red Hatchet. "Red Hatchet, help me. I would speak with you."

He got the old Shaman to stop. "I must speak to the chiefs. Is there a way I can get the chiefs to not tell all about my reading of lips?"

"Chief Walks Fast has said your father is to bring you to his lodge later to speak about that. There is nothing you can do. Go and watch what happens to an army man that lied to your chief."

Rusty went back to their lodge. He was to be there anyway. He wanted no part in the sure to come torture of the Major. He found he was tired and lay down with the first book he could put his hand on. It was the Bible. He opened and found he was on the story of Samson, so he read. It came to him that this holy book was also about killing and wars. Setting Sun came in. She had a strange look on her face. She moved till the light from a fire was on her, then she moved her lips as speaking but made no sound. Her lips said, "So it is true, you can tell what is said by looking at how one says it! You have always had that power. That is how you knew the Crow warriors were coming before seeing them!"

He looked at her, and said without speaking, "Yes." There was no reaction, so he said it again with a tiny sound. "Yes!" then again louder. He watched her smile.

"You must teach me how to do that!"

"No, it is not always a good thing and very hard to learn." He could see her look of determination, so he said, "To learn lip reading, you first must be a very strong reader of words, even in Latin," he lied. "And in the family I would need permission from Tall Elk to teach you that. I may be in trouble over not telling from the day I came here."

"There is no trouble, for you are a hero for saving the chiefs. They are talking about how to reward you as we speak." Rusty was thinking what to say when he heard a scream like he had never heard before. He pulled a blanket over his ears. Setting Sun sat next to him and put her arm around him.

"They are skinning him. It will take a long time. Do you want to go and walk away for a while? There is a fine fire to see where they are burning the wagons with chains."

He spoke softly. "They should not burn those wagons. They are proof of the trickery and lies of the army."

"Too late. I think I have a wise brother. Father says someday you will be a chief. Come, we shall walk. If we go past the pine trees, the screaming will not reach us."

"I have a big secret that I must tell the chiefs. I wish I could tell you, but must not. It might get you also in trouble. That too troubles my head."

They walked. The sounds of screaming grew fainter with passing through the pine trees.

"My brother, this may not be a good time, but I want to make you happy and more of a man."

"What do you mean?"

"May I be plain in my words, even if it makes you blush? You can say no, or even, not at this time."

"Go on. If I can stop you when I feel like doing so."

"Rusty, you are fifteen. You are very well liked by the young girls, and even girls older than you. And you must know that other braves your age get more...respect from the men in the tribe."

"I know these things, you are saying...what? Speak plain. What has this to do about blushing?"

"Please don't get angry with me, but I know you have not slept with a girl. Boys your age have..., all of them. I think you don't know how to ask, or you are afraid of making a fool the first time."

Rusty said nothing for a while, then spoke. "Let us speak of this some other time. I have more important things on my mind. See, I am not blushing. The screaming has stopped. Let us return."

"You are just like a boy, afraid to admit being afraid. Girls worry about the first time too! And the screaming will start again. One time Walks Fast and Berry Woman made a white man feel torture for six days."

When they reached the lodge, he took her arm. "I thank you for being helpful. If I could teach you to read lips, I would, but I can't."

Setting Sun now grabbed his arm. "Rusty, my brother, what I was just talking about had nothing to do with getting you to teach me! Do you think I am that...that...what is that word...de vee."

"Devious?" said Rusty. "No, I am sorry. You were not being devious. My head is not right. I am sure you mean well." To himself he thought, *Girl, your name should be Miss Devious!*

Rusty went into the lodge. Setting Sun walked away. She saw Cricket, a girl she knew would jump under a blanket with Rusty any time he asked. *He needs my help and shall have it. Was I not told to teach him Cheyenne ways the day he came here? I must plan it carefully*, she thought.

Rusty found that someone had left a book for him, but he could not read now. He set it aside. The screaming started again, but not as loud.

"He must be getting weak. Maybe I should let them see me there, but what if I am asked to torture him? Stay put, fool," he said to himself.

"Rusty, come," was all Tall Elk said.

Rusty had to hurry to stay with his father as they took a roundabout route to, not Walks Fast's lodge, but the lodge of Red Hatchet. He went inside to find the lodge was full with all the important members of the tribe including his mother, Walking Dove. Walks Fast was in the center, his moccasins and ankles were splattered with blood.

"Let Dreams A Lot...Rusty step here." He paused and let Walking Dove and Tall Elk move next to Rusty. "The people of the Clan of the Raven are grateful to Tall Elk, Walking Dove and Twisted Nose for this boy. A boy who with gifts from a great spirit that lets him hear words that his ears don't hear. He used this gift today to save his chiefs, but I don't think they would have been so foolish to go with a forked tongue trick of a lying white soldier. It is easy for me to say I was not fooled and would have got into wagons with chains, but all know this boy made sure. He protected his chiefs even if he had to tell of his gift. A gift he wisely did not tell about. We have said that of the forty horses and sixteen mules the army gave us today..." there was laughing when he said 'gave us.' He started over. "...I said forty, no! I let them have two back of the gift from the white father in a place called Washington." He stopped. Rusty could tell he was tired and lost his train of thought.

"The elders say Rusty is to have his pick of ten of those horses. He may wear two eagle feathers and is now a full brave. His age not to be...what his age is...not a problem."

Rusty didn't know what to think. He asked his father if he could speak to just him and Walks Fast. "It is important, Father!"

"If it is about your secret, you are to speak with Red Hatchet about that, but I tell you, he will want you to tell all about how you do this lip talking. The Cheyenne, unlike the white men, are truthful."

"Father, that is only a part of what I need to say. I know I should wait till Walks Fast is done with torturing the Major. Maybe I could just speak to you about what it is. Yes, of course, may I?"

"The Major dies tonight at the next torture. The village is to move the next day. The braves watching the walking soldiers will return and then we move."

116

"Father, I heard Walks Fast say he would have braves shoot buffalo to feed them."

"Our chief is a wise man. He does not want to start a war. A brave is to leave two rifles and powder ahead of the walking soldiers. They can feed themselves or starve. At first meal, talk to me about this thing that bothers your head."

* * * * * *

"Rusty, are you awake?" said Setting Sun.

"Yes, I am now. What?"

"The village is to move."

"Did you wake me for that? I knew we are to move. Maybe I will lose the book with the love story. Things get lost when moving."

"Then you did not know about Winter Rose and Running Antelope? They left tonight. They are to live as man and wife with another tribe. Running Antelope gave White Hawk twenty ponies. That is more than any I can remember."

"How can that be? They are of the same clan?"

"It happens when there is love. They will live together, no wedding ceremony. After a time together, maybe three moons, they might move back. All will know them as husband and wife. I hope this news does not make you sad. I know how you liked Winter Rose."

"Thank you. I always knew this would happen. She is two years older than me. Burned Face told me so years ago."

Cloud Woman called out. "You two, sleep or talk outside the lodge! The night is not over."

Fifteen-year-old Rusty had in his head a list of girls he would like to sleep with. He moved Winter Rose from the top of the list by drawing a line with an imaginary pen through her name. Now Voice Like A Man was the top name. He smiled to think how Setting Sun would act if she knew her name was not on the list.

At first meal, Walking Dove asked Rusty to explain to his family about his knowing what was said by looking at lips. "Please show us."

Tall Elk gave his approval with a nod. Rusty said something, then said the same thing without making a sound. "Look, watch my lips. I am saying 'The sky is blue.' See how I say it with no sound? See how when I say the same thing and speak out?" He saw they did not fully understand. He looked at Walking Dove and moved his lips only, again. "Mother, say something, while I watch, but don't make any sound. You said 'There are no clouds, we can see the stars.'" She clapped.

"My turn," said Setting Sun.

"No, I am not!" he looked around. "She asked if I was afraid of girls." Tall Elk tried. "I can't say that! Father, say something else."

"So you can read the lips of only girls? Talk, say what words were on my lips."

"Very well. Setting Sun, these are your father's words, not mine. Father said, 'Setting Sun needs Rusty to spank her many times each moon!'" All laughed, even Setting Sun. In fact she laughed too much.

Cloud Woman spoke. "Enough of game. We have a lodge to move soon. There are many things not to save or move. Give them away or pile them for others to take today. I have work to do." She left.

Rusty asked his father if they could go for a walk and speak of his problem.

It was a clear day except to the east where a cloud of dust was from the boys moving the pony and horse herds to new grass.

"So, talk, what is this problem that is so important it is for chiefs to do with?"

"You know of the lip reading skill I have. Because of it, I know where the tribe's gold is hidden. I know I should not know, but it happened. I wanted to tell you so it could be moved, but I could not tell without telling about lip reading. I was afraid you would think my not telling about that would be seen as a lie, and I would be sent away."

"How did you know? Who spoke? Who had that on his lips that you could see his words? That is more important than your knowing, unless you told where it is."

"No, I was never told. When the brave that hid the gold was telling Walks Fast, I was walking by. I try and not read lips all the time, but he was saying words that came from a story I had told about three bears, so I watched, and before I knew what it was about, I knew where the gold is hidden. We must tell Walks Fast, yes?"

"Come with me. We will do that now."

Rusty was surprised at the reaction of the chiefs. Walks Fast looked Rusty in the eye. "It is as you have told. You have told no one where the gold is?" said Walks Fast.

"Yes," said a nervous Rusty.

Walks Fast smiled and put his arm about Rusty's shoulders. He looked at Tall Elk. "You tell your son about what we agreed to before the move."

"Rusty, only three know where the gold is, you and two that are older. It was agreed days ago that one trusted young brave be told, in case something happened to the older two. You have saved us the hunt for that younger person. If you are dying for any reason, or leaving, you must find a trusted young brave to tell where that gold is. We have heard of tribes that lost wars to the whites and must live where they are told to. The Cheyenne will never let that happen. But it is wise to be ready in case. Wars can be lost." He smiled. "Even with advice from books read by a 'lost, wet, boy of ten.'"

Rusty was putting his books in a bag to move when he found the new book that had been left in the lodge after the wagons were burned. He opened the cover and read: PRINCIPLES OF WARFARE, Vol. No. 1, Infantry; West Point Manual 001. He couldn't believe his eyes. He opened to the first chapter. The heading was: Offense vs. Defense. He carefully put it back in the bag to read later. He would read it many times.

* * * * * *

The village move began. Two days later, Rusty was helping move the pony herd. He had to stop trying to use the horse Samson, as Samson always wanted to race.

The move began, the body of the skinned Major was left tied to a pole. Rusty learned this was to be a longer move than most because of the problem with the Major who tried to trick them. Rusty asked Tall Elk where some of his friends were.

"They have been sent to warn other tribes about the army lie and trick with wagons and chains. Even the Crow will be warned."

Most moves were done in two or three days. The tribe with all lodges and belongings traveled about ten miles a day. This move would be a six or more day move. Finding buffalo would decide how far they would move. The direction was southwest. Scouts rode ahead and when a good spot was found, they would stop for a night. The final stop would only be when there was game like buffalo, water from a good stream and firewood. Buffalo dung, called chips by most, would only be used while traveling.

Chapter 10

St. Joseph, Missouri, spring 1863

Waiting in the hallway of the Weaver home, Teddy was at last told by the doctor he could go to his mother.

"We miss you at the office. When will you return?"

"I don't know. It's been two weeks and that quack has no idea of what is wrong. He tells me what I know, I have trouble eating and am weak. What are the problems? Why is it that you come every day and I have to send for George? How is George doing?"

"George is like a...a king. No, a dictator. The men don't like him. He is too bossy."

"Does he get the work done? Are the wagons leaving and returning on time? Ted, I had to put George in charge. It should be that he handles the mule skinners and equipment sheds and warehouse. You meet and deal with the customers, and Gail's husband, Fred, does the books. Gail has family. Her only duty is to smile and greet new customers while they wait. Weaver & Weaver is becoming one of the best hauling firms in the Midwest."

"Mother, I am not happy. Let me go with a wagon team supplying the forts out west. I could lead a team, and we could learn firsthand about how to do things better. And I could look for Rusty."

"That would be impossible. Do you know how many miles there are out beyond Kansas?"

"I have an idea. You had a tin plate photograph made of the family before father got sick. I plan to have an artist copy Rusty and add a few years. I'll have posters printed. I could leave them in our stopping places."

"Get George to come here today after closing hours. You make one good point."

Ted was pleased when George agreed to let him go on a wagon train shipping dry goods to western forts. Ted had to settle for second in command of a train of six wagons going almost all the way to Oregon.

* * * * * *

The new village site was picked by Walks Fast and the elders; it was not near any village of Indians or routes of white wagons. Rusty was sure Walks Fast was playing it safe after his dealing with the Major that tried to trick them. The second day there, Red Hatchet sent for Rusty.

"Rusty, I thank you for telling me how you read the words on the lips that are to be said. I will speak to the chiefs and elders. This gift, or as you call it, 'a skill that can be learned,' has helped our people. I will send for you later today. Don't go far."

Later he learned that he was to speak to as many of the tribe as could be gathered at council and show how he could read lips. He must let all know how he could do it, so if they want to speak without him knowing, he should not use this gift, and they would not be considered impolite if speaking with a hand over the mouth.

Two days later Tall Elk told Rusty there would be a big council meeting. He would speak. Walking Dove saw that Rusty was dressed in his best. She also told him, "Son, you will be asked to prove what you do with words and lips is true. First you must thank the elders for naming you a full adult brave. There is talk of resentment. Never has one so young been given that honor. Be humble and don't make fun

122

of anyone when doing your lip...you call it...reading, lip reading."

Walks Fast spoke. "The scouts had picked a good site for this camp, but the buffalo have moved south. There will be another move in a few days. A move south closer to where wagons go, no one is to go near those wagons. If they are to know where the Cheyenne are, let them find us, not our people going to them to trade. The great spirit of the buffalo gives the Cheyenne all that is needed. Now Dream A Lot...Rusty will speak."

"I am grateful for the honors the elders have given me. I will do my best to prove they made a wise choice. I am to show a skill, a thing I learned in the white man's world, a thing only a few whites can do. It is like one white buffalo in an endless herd that has this skill. I say that not to boast, but so none think all whites or even a few can do this." Rusty looked around for a brave that he didn't speak to. "Gray Wolf, the brave next to you, please have him come here. I don't know his name or I would say it. Tall brave, what is your name?"

"I am called Two Arrows. What does the son of Tall Elk wish?"

"Have I spoken to you today?" asked Rusty.

"You have never spoken to me, but when I was with some hunters and you told a story to all."

"Two Arrows, the chiefs have told me to do a thing, I wish you to help me. Please go as far as I can see you, where if you speak softly, I could never hear you. Go over there. Take a brave with you. When I put up my hand, tell that brave two things that I don't know. Then send him to me."

Two Arrows spoke. "I don't understand. What am I to say?"

"Say...the name of a horse, say a number of anything, say what you think, or say the name of an Indian of another tribe. Please do it now, people are waiting."

When the brave was on the far side of a large group, Rusty had to yell, "I must see you. Get so people are not between us. There, now speak." Rusty put up his hand. He called to a brave that was halfway to him. You, Brown Bow, did you hear what he said? No! Good. Now have the brave with Two Arrows go to Chief Walks Fast."

Rusty turned to his chief and the elders. "Two arrows said, 'He has a horse named Spot On Head, he has fourteen good ponies, and he knows a Sioux brave named Shoots Coyotes.'" The brave next to Two Arrows reached the chiefs, who asked him what Two Arrows said.

"It did not make sense. He said he had fourteen ponies, one named Spot On Head, and there was a Sioux brave named Shoots Coyotes." Rusty had to do lip reading three more times, each a success. Then he was told to go. He heard whispers as he passed about not a thing to learn but a magic thing. After getting tired of being asked how he did it, he began to make up answers. "I drank from a magical stream, my mother fed me only berries for a year, or, I have an invisible bird that helps me, and even, as a baby I was dunked into a special pool." Tall Elk heard him and told him to stop. For a few days, Rusty saw people put hands in front of mouths when speaking, but that soon stopped. The village packed and moved again, this time they stopped in four days. There was good grass, a mountain nearby with trees and game, and the stream was the only one for many miles so buffalo came there.

With his status as an adult brave, Rusty went on hunts and learned to smoke a pipe.

Chapter 11

Rusty was sitting near the stream. His sister, Setting Sun, could not tell if he was awake or deep in thought.

"Hello, my all important, wise brother."

He jerked his head and stood, looked at her and rubbed his eyes. "That is a truly fine dress you have on. Are you wearing it for someone special?"

"No, just to make Cloud Woman know that I like it. What were you thinking about?"

"You have come just in time. I have a question that you could help me answer."

"What?"

"I feel a need to prove that I can really live as an Indian. That I could live with just these hands and what I have learned." He pointed to his head and held out empty palms.

"Why? What is so important about a something like that? Is there a girl you wish to...oh, what is that word, impress, that's it...yes, a girl you wish to impress?"

"No, not a girl, just me and a whole tribe. I am not just a teller of stories and reader of books. Do I need to get permission from Tall Elk to go live on my own for a while?"

"It is good you asked. No, but you must tell Tall Elk, and it would not be polite to not tell your family."

"Thank you, my wise big sister." Setting Sun was surprised and pleased at his calling her his big sister, then she saw him wink and it dawned on her he was making fun of her. She tried to kick his rear as he walked away, but fell as he saw her shadow and jumped in time. He stopped and helped her up, then to her even more surprise, gave her a hug and light kiss on a cheek.

"Just for luck, and in case something happens to me when I am alone without my rifle." Rusty was pleased that Tall Elk and Walking Dove easily understood that he would be going away for a short time and not taking any weapons, or even a knife with him.

"What you are doing is a good thing, and a going that many wise young braves have done. No one would think less of you if you carried some food so you could just travel the first few days." Walking Dove gave him a bag of pemmican that he took, as he dropped his knife.

"It is wise to be able to protect yourself from a bear or raiding tribes. You could take a rifle that you keep near at night. Count and show us how many rifle balls you take, then when you return you can show that you never used the rifle, by their count."

Rusty removed all but five lead balls from the small bag that was tied to his powder horn, and started to leave with just the rifle, powder horn, and the bag of pemmican. Tall Elk handed him a small blanket and explained that he would use it, to wrap his rifle.

Rusty was sure that the area to the north was not home to any of the smaller tribes. He had been riding there a few days before looking for elk and thinking about his plan to test himself by going primitive. He walked for all the daylight hours for four days.

This is my spot, he thought when he found a small clearing next to a stream with a large endless side hill of pine trees. While walking he had made his plans. Tools and fire were his first objectives. Then he would address his new hunger. The pemmican was long gone. He searched the streambed until he found some large rocks that were like flint. Rusty smacked the largest round rocks on smaller ones until he had some flakes with sharp edges. He used the smallest sharp flake to cut off tall stems of a tough kind of grass. Next he peeled the outer leaves and began to weave three inner stems into a kind of thin rope that he used with a willow limb to make a bow. It took a while to find the right dry wood for a twisting drill stick, and brace for his hand,

and then he split a small log of soft wood that was dry and had been cut off by beaver. He knew that the beaver would have worked on soft wood, the kind that could be used to make a fire. With a sharp wedge-shaped rock, and a bigger heavy one, he split the small beaver-cut log to give him a flat piece. It took him a while to master the bow and drill skill at making fire. The dry mouse nest from inside a hollow log worked to start his fire. He used most of the daylight hours gathering a supply of firewood.

Fishing with a spear was not successful, so he used a large flat rock to break off two limbs of a thorn tree. He picked a spot on the stream where it was only a foot from the land to a deep section of water where there was shade. Rusty moved his head over the bank so slow that to a fish it would not be a motion to warn the trout. He pinned the fish with the thorn's branches and racked it into his reach. *Fish for my first meal*, he spoke out loud to the pine trees. After he used a fleck of rock to help skin the fish, he roasted it on a green stick, and without thinking, threw the fish head and guts into the stream.

It took hours to make a stone spear point and a few arrowheads for the bow and four arrows he made from basswood. A target made of a roll of grass allowed him to practice with the bow and arrow without breaking the arrowheads. It was just before dark when he put an arrow into a rabbit. He built up his fire until he could just use hot embers to cook the rabbit. There was a loud splashing noise from the stream. It was a full grown black bear eating the fish remains. On looking closer, Rusty saw that the bear was not in good shape. You could see its skin stretched over its ribs. He yelled and the bear turned and walked away, looking back at him several times. The rifle was moved into the small hut Rusty had made with sticks and branches from a cedar tree. This bear would not be a good hunter and could be a problem, so Rusty built a larger fire each night. The next ten days went by fast as he was always busy hunting small game and picking berries. He found the berry picking so boring he wondered how the girls could stand doing it. *The girls would laugh if they saw my poor excuse of a basket made from willow sticks.* Out of a short willow tree he shot a porcupine and used its large needles on his arrows for shooting birds. There were ruffled grouse and ducks on his tree bark plate many evenings.

The stream was shaped in a curve and where the water was shallow on one side, he discovered that the stream had moved over at some time. When the water was high after a rain, there was even a flow through the older streambed. That gave him an idea. First he wove a net-like barricade of willow as wide as the stream. Next he carried rocks and piled up dirt so he could make a dam. Rusty walked back and forth along the bank as he worked out his steps. Step one was to wade and drive the fish up stream. Next he used rocks and cut poles to hold his fish barrier in place. It was hard work since he had to do it fast, but he made a dam upstream just above where he had cut a ditch into the old streambed. Soon the water was low and he had trapped more fish than he could believe were in a hundred yards of stream. The biggest dozen he threw up on the bank, and then removed the screen of willow and broke his little dam. *I can't eat all these fish.* He rolled his willow screen and put it around a small deep hole near his side of the stream. He picked most of the bigger fish that were still flopping and put them there. *Now I have a supply of fresh fish.* Two days later he went to get a fish for breakfast and saw that the two biggest fish were gone. Then he was surprised to find a well-made flint knife in the stream. *Funny I never saw that before*, he thought.

He was dragging a large dead limb for firewood to his camp when he saw the old bear stealing his fish. He ran and yelled at it, and then discovered he was too far from his hut, and his rifle was not loaded as well. He stood his ground and yelled and waved his arms at the bear. It could not make much of a groan since its jaw on one side was still hanging down. Then it charged. Rusty tripped and saw he had caught his foot on the limbs of the thorn tree. He rolled over and just in time, poked at the bear's face with the thorn limbs. It worked, and they battled for a while as the bear circled and swiped at the branch, but could not get to Rusty without the thorns sticking at his eyes and sore jaw. Frustrated, the bear left. Rusty loaded his rifle, and ate the last of his trapped fish. Just before dawn he heard the noise of wolves attacking something. With his rifle he walked in that direction and saw to his dismay the largest pack of wolves he had ever seen. A lone wolf ran off holding a black piece of hide. They were fighting over the body of a black bear. Most likely the old bear with the injured jaw. That many wolves made him nervous. He began to pack to leave when two Cheyenne braves leading a third empty pony rode out of the pine trees. The pony looked a lot like one of his.

"Welcome, Dreams-A-Lot, son of Tall Elk. Come with us. You are no longer safe here alone," said a brave who introduced himself as Lone Hawk and his friend named Man Whose Gun Kicks. Rusty was surprised to find their small village just over the pine tree ridge from his camp.

"How long have you been here?" he questioned.

"Half a moon before you came. The elders saw that you wished to be alone and told all to stay away. As the wolves began to be a problem, two braves were posted to watch for you. One, a fat belly named Beaver Foot, has a woman who likes fish. He made the trade of a knife that you could use."

"I never saw so many wolves. Are you planning a hunt? Could I join you? I have this Hawkins rifle."

"The white men that shoot buffalo for hides are leaving so much meat that the wolves and coyotes are more than ever. We sent word to your chief, Walks Fast, when you first came here. He was pleased and questioned if we could tell how long you would be here. The brave that took the message came back with a pony we were told belongs to you. There may be a reason for you to go back. The wolf hunt will not be for two days until a bright moon."

Rusty thanked Lone Hawk and his lodge with a story and was rewarded with a two-day supply of dried meat for the ride back. It only took a day-and-a-half to cover what had taken him four days walking. He was greeted by his sister, Setting Sun, who gave him a hug and asked about his efforts at living as an Indian with no tools. Before he could answer, they were joined by three young girls demanding when he was going to tell them the new story he had promised.

Rusty saw a need to cut his story telling as he began to see himself as more of an Indian warrior than just a teller of stories. His resolve was reduced by the flattery of the girls.

"I'll tell you a love story tonight, but I am about out of stories." He was in fact stuck for what he would tell and wished he had given himself more time.

Chapter 12

Rusty took a better look through his Bible and found the story of King David and Bathsheba. He told Setting Sun, "If you have some friends that would like a good story, I have a new one."

"Is it a love story?"

"In a way."

Likes To Sing called Rusty to stop and speak to him. He was with three young braves that often waited near the lodge of Tall Elk, hoping to speak to the aloof Setting Sun.

"Rusty, my sister tells that you are to read a story of love to many young squaws tonight. Share with us your magic in gathering in these love birds."

"I would help you if I could. Wait! When I am done reading, there may be some that are in a mood to be with a brave. I can, if you wish, give a signal when I am done reading."

"Yes! What signal?"

Rusty had to think quickly, he had been joking. "I shall fire a pistol, not a real loud one, just before I am done. What happens next is up to you. I must go."

Many moons before, Cloud Woman, at his asking, had made him a way to carry one of the two dueling pistols from the uncle Count of Cry A Lot. She made a thin leather holster that would fit under his shoulder. Before going to the lodge of Walks Fast that Setting Sun had talked Berry Woman into letting her use because of its size, he put a small load of gunpowder and only wadding in one of the pistols. His vest hid it from view. He used paper from a wasp nest and packed it tight to get a good, but not too loud shot. He developed the habit of being the last or near last to arrive at these readings. Setting Sun had been granted the use of the chief's lodge because Berry Woman and Walking Dove would be there.

When Rusty walked in holding the Bible, he would have been labeled a ham by today's standards.

"This is a story of a great chief. His name was David. Yes, the same David as the boy that killed the giant with his sling and a stone. He now is much older and had four wives and is chief of a great and powerful tribe. A tribe so big there was at all times some braves away fighting other lesser tribes. One day this chief, David, walked near a stream with his Shaman, a part of the stream where wives of important braves bathed. He saw a beautiful woman. "Who is that?" he asked the Shaman.

"That is Bathsheba, wife of your war chief, Uriah, from the Hittite tribe. He is away fighting the Arapaho."

"Send a message she is to come to my bed this day."

Bathsheba was fearful of not following her chief because her man Uriah was a Hittite, a far off and weak tribe. Chief David took her to his bed that night and many more." There were head shakings at this bad behavior by the crowd listening to Rusty. Then, this Bathsheba said she was with child. Chief David sent for her man, Uriah, and told him he was to rest and spend time with his wife, as a reward for his leadership in battle. Chief David learned by his spies that Uriah was sleeping outside of his lodge and sent for him.

"'Why are you not sleeping with your wife?' asked Chief David. The Hittite answered saying, 'I am well respected by the braves I lead. I eat what they eat, I sleep as they sleep, and I fight with them. They are now not with their wives and are sleeping on the ground. I am being true to them.' So Chief David sent him back to fight the Arapaho, but he told two other warriors to have Uriah be in the front of the fighting and to back off and leave him there. He was killed, and then Chief David took Bathsheba as a fifth wife. The Shaman came and told Chief David that he was no longer fit

132

to wear the feathers of a chief; he called the God and Spirits to strike Chief David with thunder and lightning. And they did!" Rusty yelled, as he fired his pistol and scared all into screams that quickly changed to screams of delight. Berry Woman looked for a bullet hole in her lodge and saw only fine bits of wasp paper drifting down. Rusty refused to retell the story a second time and let the girls make a fuss over him before leaving. Several young bucks were waiting after he was done. Setting Sun and Walking Dove walked Rusty back to their lodge, both wondering why he was not going into the brush with one of the young squaws that would have gone with him, if he had read their signs, and not a book.

* * * * * *

Setting Sun saw Pigeon Girl, the wife of Burned Face, at the stream while filling water bags made from Buffalo stomachs.

"Pigeon Girl, may I speak with you?"

"Please. Is there anything I can help you with?"

"These words are just for us, and maybe Burned Face. It is about my brother. May I come and speak at your lodge after I take this water to Cloud Woman?"

"Yes, I will make us some coffee. Do you want my husband there?"

"Not until we speak. It is he that I need, but first must ask your advice."

"This sounds interesting. I will rush back."

Setting Sun found Cloud Woman not there. Her mother, Walking Dove was. She decided to seek her advice.

"Mother, you must know your son, my brother, is at an age where he should have been with a woman. He does not know some of his friends tease me about it. I think he is both shy and fearful of making a mistake. I know many girls that would bed him after his storytelling. He can read lips, but not the signs young squaws give when they are interested. Shall I give him a push?"

"Are you trying to be helpful, or mean? I know how you like to tease him. This is not a thing to tease about. I, too, have heard squaws ask if he likes girls. Some think it strange that after reading his love story he was not under a blanket with a girl every night. How would you push him?"

"I would ask his best friend, Burned Face, to give him advice on how, and drop a hint with a girl that would, and maybe arrange for them to be alone. I only mean to help. Do you think I should?"

"Yes, but be careful. He is still a boy no matter what the chiefs have said."

Pigeon Girl agreed that Burned Face would be glad to give such advice. He would be there soon. With that, Setting Sun stopped a child running by and asked him to have Rusty come to the lodge of Burned Face. He should be fishing at the stream, or reading a book while fishing. Burned Face came in and heard the request.

"You want me to teach Rusty about THAT!" He smiled, thought a minute, and said, "Maybe there is way. I must be alone with him. He does know I am to speak to him about it?"

"Yes," lied Setting Sun. "I'll go and get him now," she said as she started to leave thinking, *Just how am I going to tell my brother that his best friend would be happy to give advice on bedding a girl?*

Before she could leave, Rusty entered the lodge.

"I was told to come here. What for?"

The girls looked at Burned Face who picked up his long rifle. "I was wondering if we can go hunting soon." He removed the ramrod and ran it down the barrel.

"Are you loading that here?" asked Rusty.

"No, I was just practicing cleaning my rifle. See, first you put oil on your hand and gently run your hand all over it, all over it, gently. Then push the rod in, then you pull it out, not all the way out, push it in, pull it out, many times." He was having trouble keeping from laughing as he spoke. The girls were rolling on the floor giggling. Burned Face looked to the girls with a smiling questioning look.

"Have you all been eating loco weed?" said Rusty. "I know how to clean a rifle. You may not, as I see no patch with oil on that rod, so what are you doing other than pushing it in and pulling it out?"

"My friend, I..." he stopped and could not speak.

"My brother, your friend is trying to tell you about a something, but while he knows how, he is not sure you do. Just remember what he has said."

"All he said is, push it in, and pull it out, over and over."

This caused the girls to break into fits of laughing. Even Burned Face laughed and crawled out of the lodge. Rusty left shaking his head.

Setting Sun learned that Long Bow, who lived alone, was away for a few days. His small lodge would be empty. Setting Sun asked Rusty what he was going to do after the evening meal.

"I was given a new book. It does not look like a book with a story. A brave found it along the trail used by wagons. It looks like a book of numbers for some business. I plan to study it. Why do you ask?"

"I might need you to do a something." She moved because of her failing to suppress a giggle.

She needs to let me teach her more skills with words. She is always saying 'a something.' It is her word for too many things, he thought.

An hour later a boy came to Rusty saying he was to go to the lodge of Long Bow and wait inside. Rusty pushed open the door flap. Light came from a tallow lamp made from a buffalo horn.

"Hello, Rusty," said Voice Like A Man, who was sitting up on a robe wearing only a few white flowers in her hair.

A stunned Rusty paused. *This has to be the doing of Setting Sun.* His angry feelings of her butting into his life were no match for the urges of a male towards what was there waiting for him. She guided him with care into their joining. He was just getting going, when if anyone was walking near, they would have heard him laugh and exclaim, "Push it in, pull it out, the cleaning rod!"

The next morning, Rusty rode out meeting with some braves to hunt antelope. He was met by Burned Face and three braves, all holding rifles who were running the ramrods in and out for his eyes.

Chapter 13

In what is now Wyoming, there were two groups of wagons going west. The first group was six wagons of gold seekers heading for northern California. They were led by a promoter known as Grant Newman. Not a soul among them had even been west of St. Louis. What they knew of Indians was from barroom tales and eastern newspapers. They were four days ahead of the six freight wagons of Weaver & Weaver carrying dry goods for the stores at three western forts, with Ted Weaver as second in command. The wagon master, and a seasoned trail boss, was Matt London who had once traveled to the west coast with Kit Carson.

The Cheyenne of Walks Fast's tribe were ten miles from one point of the trail the wagons used. A party of ten hunters, some young, had just shot four buffalo. They were cutting the meat and loading it on travois to pull back to the village when they heard the wagons coming near. A single brave rode to investigate. He was shot on sight by a nervous would-be gold prospector that had a good long range rifle. Six of the remaining braves rode hard at the wagons; two had the new Henry rifle which gave them confidence. They only saw the drivers of the wagons and not the load of armed men inside. Five of the six were shot, two were wounded and returned. The wagons did not stop nor did any go after the Indians because there was only the horse of Grant Newman, so the Indians rode off with the dead and wounded, not meat. There was sadness and anger among the many well-armed braves. The chiefs agreed on a retaliatory raid on these wagons. A raid with two hundred braves.

The scouts reported that the six wagons that had shot the Cheyenne hunters were near a river crossing. An attack was set when half the wagons were in the water. Rusty was with the attack braves that would go around and cut off any retreat from the last wagons.

Ted Weaver had volunteered to ride in the last wagon because of dust, not a chore most welcomed. He wanted to show that even if he was an owner, he was no better than the mule skinners he hired. Many of the wagon drivers were veterans of the Civil War, some that were wounded, others that grew tired of the senseless dying and found their way west. A few were the scrapings from jails and bars. There were two men per wagon, and all were well armed. Ted had listened to the experienced Matt London and carried trade beads and iron cookware to barter for safe passage.

When the Cheyenne attacked, there was no chance to barter, little chance to fight. When three of the six wagons were fording the stream, the Cheyenne attacked. The attack to the rear was just a second later at the river. Ted jumped from the wagon and, holding a pistol, crawled into a low spot and hid. The shooting was over almost as fast as it started. No one among the Cheyenne noted that there were six wagons with two men on each. Only Rusty did when he started to count the scalpings. He rode back past the last wagon. He was looking in the low spot and saw Ted, who shot at him and missed.

"Ted, for God's sake, don't shoot. It's me, Rusty!" Rusty had to think fast. He was riding Samson. "Come here, Ted, jump up with me before you are shot. What are you doing here? Wait, how is Mother?" Ted was at a loss for words.

"We...I have been looking for you!"

Rusty had to think fast. "Ted, ride east. Go now!" Rusty jumped off Samson hitting his hand hard on the horse's rump. As Ted rode off, Rusty yelled, "Tell Mother I'll be home next year." The first brave to get there was Gray Wolf. He started to go after Ted.

"Wait, stop, help me," Rusty pretended to be hurt. That gave Ted all the lead Rusty knew he would need riding Samson.

"What is this all about? You let that white man take your horse, and you are not hurt?"

"That was my white brother. I think we have attacked the wrong wagons."

The wagons were at first stripped of goods, then it was ruled by White Hawk to take three wagons and their goods back to the village. Running Bear looked at the guns taken and said, "These are not the ones that shot our hunting braves. We have killed the wrong white men. Let us take all wagons and bodies and hide them." His word was listened to, and after much looking, a riverbank that was about to cave in was chosen as a place to hide the bodies.

When Rusty admitted that one man had gotten away, White Hawk walked away angry, not giving Rusty a chance to tell why. The wagons were taken back away from the trail and once emptied, burned, and the metal parts dug into the ground, except for some bits of iron that Rusty said to save for Iron Hand.

"Father, I have to say the horse Samson is gone. I will gladly give you eight of mine. The four you traded for him, and four more as what he was worth."

"I told you to ride him on this raid. Talk no more of giving me your horses. Was he hit by a bullet or stolen during the fighting?"

"I gave him away. I had no choice."

"Talk, explain!"

"I let my brother ride him to save his life."

"What brother?"

"My white brother, Ted, who of my two brothers was close to me. He was one of the wagon drivers. I found him hiding in a ditch. He is a Weaver of the freight line that uses wagons. To save his life, I could only think to let him ride away on my, I mean, your horse. So you see, I owe you for Samson. He was, I mean, is my white brother, what else could I do?"

"Rusty, you have saved many Cheyenne lives by talking miners into giving up their guns, by sharing book words on how to fight better to some braves, and by reading words on mouths and maybe saving me and chiefs from a trap. You think I care about one horse? And a horse that will not train to win long races? I think you have two white brothers. If the other comes here, tell me, and you shall ride an old worthless horse that day." Then Tall Elk hugged Rusty and laughed.

"Your sister tells me I am not to clean my rifle when you are around or you will think I am teasing you. Do I want to know what that is about?"

"Father, in this village, you will know if I tell you or not. I should make a bet with Setting Sun on how long until you know."

"If it is a funny thing, then tell me as the price for giving away my horse Samson."

It took Rusty a long pause to decide if he could tell his father about the ramrod incident. *He will hear anyway*, thought Rusty.

"My sister, meaning well, was not sure I would know what to do with my...I mean how to...I mean how to...with a woman...in bed. I think she asked Burned Face to tell me. All he did was to keep cleaning his rifle. He would keep pushing the ramrod in and pulling it out. This while he, Setting Sun and Pigeon Girl laughed. I pretended to not know what he was speaking of. Of course, I knew!"

Tall Elk thought a minute. "Yes, I'm sure you know how...I mean knew..., I must go."

Rusty was sure he heard his father laughing once he was out of the lodge.

* * * * * *

Teddy Weaver rode for his life. He had a hard time riding bareback, but the big horse held a steady, even pace. He had a death grip on its long mane. He saw that the sun was behind him, and the horse was staying on a trail of wagon ruts.

There is a wagon train that was not far behind ours. I have to make it there. He knew he should get off and walk the horse, but being as it was not his horse and he was riding without a saddle, he dared not get off. He tried to get it to slow to a walk, but it stayed at a steady clip.

As a precaution, White Hawk had sent scouts far in all directions for this attack. He did not want any wagons with soldiers to join the fight. One of these braves saw this man riding away. He had to be coming from the attack. This white man had no weapon. The brave rode to get close and use his tomahawk. Before Teddy saw him, Samson smelled or heard his pony. When the brave would get close, Samson would run faster, pulling Ted out of harms reach. Frustrated and wanting to use his Tomahawk, the brave stayed with the race. He never got close, and when his pony began to tire, he slowed and reached for his bow. Ted and Samson rounded a curve, went over a hill, and found a wagon train of forty wagons heading towards them. The brave shot an arrow that missed and turned back.

Two of the wagons belonged to Weaver & Weaver. Ted was able to get supplies and a drive to escort him back to the next fort. He had to borrow a saddle. But when he tried to put it on Samson, the horse ran off. He had to take a horse and sign a paper that Weaver & Weaver would pay for the horse. At the fort he gave a report about the attack. The army officer was not happy that he had no idea what tribe had raided the wagons.

* * * * * *

George was furious about the loss. "I let you go one time and look what happened."

"George! Did you hear me? Rusty is alive. He is an Indian. He was dressed like one. He helped me escape. He saved my scalp and life! He yelled to tell Mother he will come home in a year. I am only here because Mother is sleeping. I can't wait to tell her. Five years, or is it six, and he is still alive. You should see him. He is bigger, his hair is braided like a girl, down to here. His freckles are almost all gone. I could not be sure with the war paint.

"Oh, good morning, Gail. Rusty is alive. I saw him. He saved my scalp! Indians, not a bear, must have taken him when we were on the rafts. When will he come home? He said in a year. No, I don't know why. No, I don't know what tribe. Wait till Mother hears. Don't cry. You girls always cry when glad or sad."

"Teddy, George, Mother just passed away. She is dead! I was with her. She just made a face, said a word in German, and closed her eyes. There is so much to do. I think the first thing is how many days shall Weaver & Weaver close out of respect?"

"If I know our mother, she would say no more than we have to. We will close the rest of this week. I will spread the word. We close at six today," said George.

"George, this is Thursday! No. I say we close till this day next week," said Ted. "What do you think, Gail?"

"I'm the president. We will be open Monday. I'll call the undertaker for a funeral on Saturday," said George.

"Gail, you and I are two-thirds of Weaver & Weaver. It would not be proper to open on the Monday after a Saturday funeral."

142

"Teddy, George may be right. You know how Mother is, I mean was. George, if we can get everything done, then Monday will be acceptable with me. I'll go back to the house and start doing what has to be done. No, I'll go see Aunt Kathy. She's been through this before."

"What are you marking that calendar for, Ted?"

"George, you know what Mother's will says. Rusty has one year from today to claim his inheritance. That's one-fourth of Weaver & Weaver."

"Do you think after all the work I've put into making this company, I will give that much to a...a renegade Indian, a killer? Why didn't he just take a horse and ride home? Did you report to the army that he was part of the Indians that attacked our wagons?"

"George, how could I? He is our brother. We don't know if he could get away from them, or even if he was part of that attack. Maybe he was there to save white people and got there too late. Don't you tell the army about him!"

"Ted, you are right, Rusty is still our brother. We will not worry about him until he is here. We have work to do. I am going to see the new captain of the cavalry. I want to see if we can hire patrolled rebel soldiers as wagon drivers. They would know how to fight. We can't afford to keep losing teams and drivers." *I wonder if they hang renegades?* he thought.

* * * * * *

The horse, Samson, was trotting as it followed the wagon ruts leading back toward where it had been with Rusty. It had to make a detour for water, returning to the direction it wanted only to find the way blocked by a ten-mile long herd of buffalo. The horse grew tired of waiting for the buffalo to pass and began to cut through the end of the herd. It found the horns of the big bulls too many and too close, and stood waiting for them to pass. He was at last at the end of the buffalo. His ability to move still blocked, the horse was unable to move fast when the wolves bit at its legs. Samson fought his way out into the open, with a pack of many wolves that were trying to bring him down. Kicking and running, he broke clear of most, with one wolf holding onto a back leg. He shook that one free and gave it a kick with his hind legs that broke its back. Once a distance from them, he rolled in dust and ran west and north.

Gray Wolf saw Setting Sun walking. He was on a pony. "Setting Sun, tell Tall Elk and Rusty that the big horse called Samson has come back and joined Tall Elk's other pony herd. It has scars, maybe from wolves. He will want to know," then he rode off.

When Tall Elk learned about Samson, he sent for Twisted Nose and Rusty. Twisted Nose got a message about the horse injured by wolf bites. Rusty met them at the herd. They could tell the horse was pleased to see Rusty, who had come with the last sugar in their lodge.

Twisted Nose had a cream he smeared on the wounds and said they would soon heal. He looked at Rusty who was letting Samson lick his hand.

"Rusty, tell us where this horse has been by looking at his lips." Then they all laughed.

* * * * * *

"Cloud Woman, please don't feed my brother so much food. He is to read a story later to my friends and if he eats too much, he will get tired and won't be able to...do it a second time..., I mean tell the story more times." Then she laughed at her slip.

Cloud Woman looked Setting Sun in the eye. "I know of what you speak. You are either a good sister or putting your nose in where it should not be." That said while she pinched Sun's nose hard. "And I will say how much he eats; he is too thin. I can't make him grow anyway but up!"

At age fifteen, according to his calendar, Rusty was an inch under six feet and weighed about one hundred and thirty at most. Rusty retold the story of young David and his sling to please Setting Sun. He made a point of saying how it was like when his sister hit a Crow in the head with a stone from her sling, and that proved that his stories from this Bible book were true. Then he told the story of Chief David and Bathsheba, this time giving the Shaman a larger part using some of what the Bible gave as an example, and then he told the story of Samson and Delilah. He made Samson a great storyteller that crowds of young women followed. Rusty made more of a tale of his fighting the Apache with the jawbone of a mule adding to the part of Delilah many young girls throwing themselves on Samson's grave because he was such a great lover. He was walking back to the lodge when Voice Like A Man stopped him. She wrapped a blanket around him and whispered in his ear.

"Rusty, I am very grateful for your storytelling. I am telling that my father has been given ten ponies and I am to wed. It is a brave I like and I am happy. I want you to be happy and so...," She ducked from under the blanket and the girl Cricket took her place who whispered in his ear, "Stand still. Setting Sun is coming. When she is gone, let us go to a private place." Later, she wanted to know if he would join her again some night, late at night.

"How can we meet without the whole village knowing?"

"I, too, am tired of the whole village knowing what I am doing, even before I do it!" That made her laugh. He worked out a signal with a piece of fishing line.

A moon later, Burned Face asked him, "How is it that the word is my shy friend is with young girls many nights? What is your secret?"

"I will tell you. In the land of the Cree, at a trading post, I used a penny to buy some fishing line. That was a great investment."

Walking Dove was also wondering about a piece of fishing line she found one morning going from outside the lodge to where Rusty slept. She asked Setting Sun.

"My brother likes to go late at night with a girl. If she comes, she pulls the string. It is tied to his foot. It wakes him. They go swimming, or walking, or, you know what."

"Maybe you pushed him too far!" said Walking Dove. "But I don't think so. He smiles a lot, and Cloud Woman says he eats more as well. Do you know how many different ones pull that string?"

Setting Sun answered, "Maybe six, maybe eight, ones he reads to mostly. I am told he never has learned how to read the signs that a girl is interested and willing, but with his string it does not matter."

* * * * * *

Tall Elk spoke at first meal. "The chiefs are making a change. There is little danger from the soldiers, and our horse herd is so large we have to move the village more than before. Until winter, the village will split. Both will move, but not to be too near each other. I am named chief of one half. We have sent scouts to look for two new places, within a day or two of each other. Chief Walks Fast wants to see Rusty this morning. I don't know what for; it must not be important."

"I have heard that Winter Rose and Running Antelope are coming back. Will they be with our village?"

"White Hawk will be with our village. Running Bear and Twisted Nose with Chief Walks Fast's village. It should be that they will want to be with us, but no one can say. It is their choice."

Rusty knew Setting Sun missed her friend Winter Rose. Both would have a parent figure in a different village. Winter Rose was the niece of White Hawk. Running Antelope was the son of Twisted Nose.

"Rusty, come, sit. We will smoke." Rusty hated to smoke, but could not say so. "Son of Tall Elk, this split of our village will only be until winter. That is four moons from now. I have this. It was saved for you to use if needed." He handed Rusty the uniform of the major that he had skinned. I want you to have Berry Woman fit it to you. There may be a time when we might like to have a Major of Cavalry, one that, thanks to storytelling, could find words to fool soldiers with. If you wish, you may ask Cloud Woman to make the changes. Berry Woman or Hands That Sing are the best, but Berry Woman says some years ago she remembers you making a blushed face when she fitted you with black clothes. Do you remember?"

"Yes, I was but a boy then. I would like to have Berry Woman make this uniform my size. Shall I come later today? Oh, was that all you wished to speak of?"

"Just that I wish you and your sister will visit between villages, and you to bring your books to read. You may go now."

"Is that all he wanted?" said Setting Sun. "It was the reading. Don't you think?"

"I have heard that the Sioux had a missionary man stay with them, then he left. He had his wife with him. A man like that might be better; he could teach you as I can't, no insult meant."

"Rusty, I know all I need. I am sure I can trust you with a big secret. You have proven good at keeping them. If you want to hear it, go with me for a walk to the stream."

There were ducks and geese in the stream. They were not afraid of the children playing in the shallow water. They sat on a bank and Rusty joked about the time his sister and friends tickled him. He waited for her to speak.

"Rusty, you are fifteen and I be sixteen. I can get the money my father Quinn left me in a bank in Quebec, but I don't have to go to there. I have learned I can get it in New York, but must wait some days."

"What do you want with that money?"

"I trust you to not tell. I plan to go to see my uncle in the place of my father's birth, Ireland. I want to see it before I become a married woman and have children. If I wait, I'll never go."

"When will you go? Soon it will be too cold to travel."

"No, I will wait till spring. Will you go with me?"

"Me? I will not be sixteen till next fall. I gave my word I would stay till then."

"I was there when you spoke those words, and Father said a man should not be held to what was said by a boy. The chiefs have made you a man. So the promise does not hold you. If you like, go just to New York and I get on a ship. Then go to see your white family. I would pay for you to go there by ship or riverboat. Think about it. These words are only between us!"

"That you can be sure of. I will think about it. I have all of a long winter and still some of this fall."

Rusty was called at the lodge of Chief Walks Fast. Berry Woman was waiting for him. She was the only one there.

"I have here the uniform of the major that was skinned for lying. You must put it on. Take off your breechcloth, it will be in the way. This time I will not look. You are no longer a little boy," she said with a chuckle, as she gave him the pants and turned away.

She waited until he had them on and tapped her. She had a stick cut with a slot. It was very much like his real mother's clothespins. She pinched the pants to his size and held them there with the stick, then marked with a soft white stone. The same was repeated on the sides of the pants. She let him dress back into his breechcloth before trying on the major's coat. It had been cut up the back two times by the knives of angry squaws the day he was skinned.

"I did not sew the cuts because I would have to make it smaller." These cuts made it difficult for her to fit it to him. She looked out and called to a girl that was bringing firewood to her lodge.

"Come here, Eyes Down, I need you just for a little." Rusty was looking down at the time and at first saw a very comely young girl. Then he saw a face that was a mass of scars, and eyes disfigured so they only looked down. She seemed very shy. Berry Woman had the girl hold the cut back while she overlapped the front and marked where to replace the brass buttons. The girl left and Rusty asked about her.

"I have never seen that girl? What happened to her face?"

"She was small and tried to load and shoot a rifle with too much gunpowder. It blew up and took off skin on her face. She is a good girl, and shy. Too bad about her looks."

"How is it I never see her? What does she do all day?"

"She spends much time with your mother, Cloud Woman, doing beads on dresses. And she goes out at night. It was strange she came by today. Maybe she saw you and wished you would invite her to hear you read."

"Would you do that for me? The next time I read to young girls, I will tell you, and you can make her come to hear. I will tell Setting Sun to have no one make fun of her face. Send for me when this soldier's uniform is ready."

Rusty went to see a squaw that painted pictures. Her name was Mirror Hands.

"What does the son of Tall Elk want from this old squaw? No, I will not come at night and pull on your string!" Then she laughed.

How does the whole village always know all about me? thought Rusty.

"Mirror Hands, could you make a face mask? A mask of softened deerskin, tanned to the darkness of real skin, and painted with a smile, and so made as to be pleasant to look at, made to wear over the face of a girl, a girl like Eyes Down?"

"So you lit a candle and saw her one night. She is more shy than even you were at first. I can make that, but what makes you think she will wear it?"

"I will find a way. Send for me, and I will give you a gift for making it."

"I believe she had such a mask her father made years ago, but it was as ugly as her scars. She only wore it till he died."

* * * * * *

"There is to be a short move, and there is to be a buffalo hunt before the village splits," said Tall Elk.

Rusty planned carefully for the hunt. He would use the Colt six-shot rifle and not the more powerful, but single-shot Hawkins. He tested the Colt .44 rifle with a great charge of gunpowder until sure that charge was safe, but the most he dared use. He made a new measuring cup from a very large acorn.

A very angry Setting Sun saw him getting ready for the hunt and kicked at his bag of powder and lead balls.

"Sorry to take it out on you, brother. Father says I am not to hunt, I must be a skinner and meat cutter like the other squaws. I can outshoot and outride many of the braves that will be shooting buffalo!"

Rusty sat next to her. "Does not a single buffalo, a bull at times, run from the herd and put squaws in danger? Would it not be wise for a squaw to have a rifle by her side? Who could question that? That Hawkins rifle hanging there will cry tears of oil if not taken on the hunt. Do you know a squaw that is a good, no, a great shot that could keep that rifle by her side? This brave is only going to carry the Colt rifle." By now they both were smiling at his remarks.

"I will show you a trick." Rusty opened a book of numbers and tore out a page and wrapped it around his finger. He crimped it on a .58 caliber rifle ball from the bag for the Hawkins. Next he measured gunpowder into the paper, twisted it shut, and put a percussion cap in the last part before folding it over. "With a few of these you don't have to carry a powder horn and bag of balls and caps."

"Let's make five," she said.

"Yes, but three will be one more than you need."

Rusty rode the horse Samson. He hung his javelin around his shoulder like the way soldiers sling a rifle. He carried the Colt rifle in his hand. Knife and extra powder and balls in a bag were tied to his belt.

"How many buffalo are you going to kill?" joked Burned Face as they waited for the signal that the medicine man was ready for them to start.

Rusty knew his friends would recognize his words as humor and not bragging when he said, "I have six shots for six buffalo. I shoot with rifle and finish with spear!"

Running Antelope smiled and said, "You will read us a story for each of the six you don't kill?"

"Yes, as long as I don't have to read a love story and you make my feet wet with tears."

Rusty and his friends were told to ride to the back behind the herd and when the shooting starts they may shoot, but should try and keep the herd as near the village as possible. Others in the front would be doing the same. Rusty's horse, Samson, would not let other ponies pass him, so Rusty went to the far end riding around his friends till he heard the first shots. As he closed on the running buffalo, a small bunch split and crossed a ridge heading away from the village. He pushed Samson after them, only to ride over the hill where a pack of wolves were dogging a group of six buffalo that included a limping old cow. At the sight of the wolves, Samson reared up and dumped Rusty. He fell hard. Samson ran off leaving Rusty on the ground. He was picking up the rifle when pain told him his arm was broken. It was the same left arm broken in the same place. The wolf pack leader stopped his running off at the sight of an Indian. This Indian was on the ground. He turned back. Rusty, holding the rifle with one hand, fired a quick shot. The shot chased off the wolves. He fired three more times at the running wolves, doing a better job of resting the rifle with an elbow on the ground. With his sixth shot, he saw a wolf fall. He stood and found the best, or least painful way to hold the broken arm was to let it hang straight down. He was walking towards the village when Running Antelope rode up.

"We heard six shots. Where are the six buffalo?"

"There is one dead wolf and one clumsy Rusty with a broken arm. No buffalo. There is a horse that is to be traded. I will walk back to see the medicine man about this arm. At least today he will have fresh rawhide to bind the break with. Will you pick up the wolf I shot? His fur looked good."

"If that arm is broken, let me give you a ride. Then I'll come back for the wolf."

"No, my friend, I am sure it will hurt less if I walk."

"I will stay with you for a way. I don't want anything to happen to our new storyteller, you know, the one that owes us braves six stories."

Rusty stopped at their lodge and got the leather arm shield that helped with the last broken arm.

"I don't think I know a boy that keeps breaking the same arm. Give the other arm a chance," joked the medicine man, White Weasel. Rusty bit a stick at the pain as his arm was felt. "Were you wearing the rifle shield as before?"

"No, I find it is too hot, and if I am wearing a long sleeved shirt of buckskin, I don't need it. The whole village is at the buffalo hunt. When I can find someone to send, I will boil some willow bark and make a broth to help with the pain."

"Wait, see that small boy? Send him to the lodge where the women do the beading. There may be a girl there, her name is Eyes Down."

"Yes, she may be there. I will send him to get her."

"Tell her it is for me."

Rusty sat outside of the lodge in the sun waiting for the rawhide on his arm to shrink and the village to return from the hunt. The willow bark tea made him lightheaded, but there was not as much pain.

"White Weasel said this break will take longer to heal," he told Walking Dove who rode her pony right up to the lodge.

"They said my Rusty had broken his arm again. Have you seen White Weasel?"

"Yes. He did what he could. I must not use it for two moons or more this time. The horse, Samson, was scared by wolves and threw me before I was ready for his rearing at wolves. I shot a wolf, but no buffalo."

"Your sister shot three and has been told that she must skin and cut two of them alone for doing so. She had your rifle. Did you know that?"

"Yes, I even suggested she take it, and I hinted she might shoot one that got too close to the skinning squaws. If my arm was not broken, I would help her. She will be all night."

"Don't worry about Setting Sun. If I know her, she will have help. I will make you a tea of willow bark for your pain."

"Only to take later. I have had too much now. The inside of my head is fuzzy."

At the dancing after the hunt, Rusty sat and tried to think what stories he would tell the braves. Running Antelope told him it was in jest and he would not hold Rusty to the boast. Rusty knew his words had spread and told all that he would have six good stories for them, but his arm had to heal a little. At the feasting and dancing after a successful hunt, he saw that Setting Sun was not there, and some of the young braves that wanted her were also missing. Rusty walked to the edge of the village. In the distance he could see the light of many fires. All the bones could not be taken care of in one day, so after a hunt, some braves rode around all night keeping wolves and coyotes and other scavengers away. He was glad that the rifle he loaned to Setting Sun was not back in its place. She would have it, but if what he was told was right, she was down to her last shot. He saw Gray Wolf walk from where the ponies were hobbled.

"Gray Wolf, did you see my sister? Are you going back to the killing area?"

"Don't worry about her, she will be back soon. Six braves are helping her, each trying to prove he is the best at skinning and cutting. Have you seen Tall Elk?"

"No, I have been looking for him since the hunt. I want to tell him about the horse Samson."

"You won't find him. He had to ride and see for himself what some scouts saw. I don't know what, but it is a thing to be worried about. He knows about your arm."

"I left Setting Sun with my rifle. She may only have one shot. I would feel better if I could send her powder and balls."

"Don't worry. As I said, she has many braves with her. They have rifles. And she has no more powder and lead balls. She shot at a wolf with her last shot. None will give her any powder because they told her not to shoot and scare the ponies that were near. I go to eat and return to riding around for the night. You picked a good time to break an arm, or you, too, would be riding instead of dancing."

Those remarks bothered Rusty. *I am trying hard to carry my load, to do my duty and not be just a storyteller to girls and squaws. And he knows I don't like to dance. It is so boring. My stomach is talking and it feels like the willow bark tea is to blame. I must eat!* he told himself.

The broken arm was tied to his chest making it difficult cutting meat with one hand, until some girls saw his problem. Then he was being teased by the braves as a group of girls were feeding him.

At morning, Cloud Woman asked, "Rusty, you have not said anything about your wolf skins. Don't you want them?"

"Skins, like in more than one?"

"You had too much willow bark tea. Running Antelope and Gray Wolf came to me with the two wolves you shot. Good shooting for a boy with a broken arm. They are fine pelts."

"Where are they? Did you skin them?"

"Yes, you could not with one hand. They are drying over by all the buffalo hides. Go and see."

Rusty found it boring with the broken arm. He read and re-read the army book on Infantry Warfare. He made a list of stories to read to the young braves. He would do three a night for two nights.

"Running Antelope, with my arm tied like this, I am not to ride. If you will get the braves to my lodge tonight, I will read three stories. Yes, I may ask Setting Sun to hold my book and turn the pages."

"No, I will not! I have other things to do. You should have asked me before saying I would help you read. If I am there, they won't pay attention to you," she said with a smile. "But I will find you someone who will."

"No, don't bother. When I think it over, I can hold the book and turn pages like this." He used his thumb as if he had a book. Rusty had forgotten that he was going to tell stories, but liked to fake that they were from a book. He had learned long before that book stories went over better than those he made up. So he pretended to be reading most of the time.

"Berry Woman wants you," said Walking Dove. "I will walk with you. Does the arm still hurt? I see you make a face of pain when sleeping."

"Yes, it hurts some. I think this break is a bigger one than before. Samson is a big horse, and I fell a long way. Maybe in one more moon it will be so I can take off these boards he tied on over the rawhide." White Weasel had placed two flat boards as a splint when he saw the arm move when Rusty walked.

"Stay and help," Berry Woman said to Walking Dove. "I have the Major's uniform for Rusty. I was going to hold it up to him because of his arm, but with your help we can put it on most of him."

The Rusty of this day was not as shy as he was at first, and he had little choice. Walking Dove held the pants and he dropped his breechcloth and with help, stepped into them. His good arm was put into the coat and it was pulled over his broken arm. Both women fastened the buttons. Then, to his surprise, Berry Woman put on a black belt and pistol holster and a big white army hat. All were clean and shiny. He asked for a mirror.

"Thank you. This is fine. Walks Fast is right, there may be a time when I could fool the soldiers and find a way to save Cheyenne lives. I want to walk around wearing this."

"Yes, it will impress the girls," said Berry Woman.

"No! I need many braves to see me in this uniform. If we are fighting the soldiers, I don't want to get an arrow stuck in me!"

"Before you go, see this. Mirror Hands sends it to you." It was the face mask he had her make for Eyes Down. "The girl refused to wear it."

"Mirror Hands should not have tried to give it to her. I was working on a plan to have my sister help me invite her to hear me tell a story, and she could come if she had the mask."

Walking Dove looked at Berry Woman and said, "Leave it here. We will find a way, but first a question. What is your interest in Eyes Down? She is sixteen and the older brother she lives with is trying to get her a husband. Except for her face, she is lovely. I hope your interest in her is not about your string."

"No, Mother, I only saw her once. She looked so sad and left out. I have had those feelings, too. Yes, help me to get her to wear it. I think once she does for a while, all will get used to it."

Rusty wore the uniform for the next two days, then put it away. The teasing by his young friends stopped when he explained his reason for wearing it.

Chapter 14

"Rusty, my uncle, White Hawk, would speak with you. Please follow me," said Winter Rose.

"This is the way to my lodge. Is White Hawk there?"

"No, but your book is, and he wants you to read from it to him and Running Bear. The book from the soldier's wagon all about making war. He has heard you have it. And after the good words on fighting you gave to the young braves before the raid on the Crow, he will listen to you."

Rusty stopped for the army manual from West Point and followed her to the lodge of the warrior Running Bear.

White Hawk saw the book and spoke. "Then it is true, the foolish white soldiers put words on paper how they are going to fight even before a battle! We would like you to read this book to us now, if you have the time, or later if not."

Rusty used his good hand to point to his arm in a sling. "I have lots of time. There is little I can do. It will be more useful if I tell you in Cheyenne what this book says instead of trying to read it to you." He saw by the look of their faces they were not sure his approach would do what they wanted, so he said, "I'll read and you will see." He started on the first chapter, Defense vs. Offense. The writer of the book, a retired general named Cunningham, began with a long paragraph about his qualification and definitions of terms.

White Hawk stopped him. "Tell us in your words the way the white soldiers would fight from this book."

Rusty started with defense vs. offense.

"If you attack a village of enemy, your attack is an offense, and the enemy is on the defense. If your attack is by all braves rushing at the enemy as soon as they get there, and they rush to fight you the same way, soon both are on offense. But if the enemy were to make a stand, hiding behind trees and gathering around their chief and best warriors, soon their defense would have an advantage over your offense. A brave firing his bow or rifle standing shoots better than a brave riding a horse. The white man's army book says that if the defense is prepared, it has a three-to-one advantage." He saw that this point was not clear. "The book says it will take three braves on offense to defeat the one brave that is fighting a good defense, like behind a tree, and they are running at him where he can shoot at them. This gets to the point the writer of this book makes; that wars are won by fighting always with an advantage—your strong points against enemies' weak points.

"Here, look at my fingers as I use them as warriors. If the soldiers attacked your village, they would not start to fight until they get to rifle range. They would line up like this with their horses behind them. This is this front facing you. The sides of their line is called their flanks. There they are weak. If you rush and take weapons and charge them as soon as each brave can, you are really using offense against their defense, and you lose the fight."

White Hawk held up a hand to stop Rusty. "Let us hold this book. I now believe it is strong medicine and we would hold it while you speak, so the book's power goes to us. Show how to fight this line of soldiers facing our village." Rusty gave him the book and both men held it.

He again used his hand and fingers as soldiers and Indian braves and demonstrated the advantages of a flank attack on the side of the soldiers. "When the village is attacked like this, rush, take weapons, but retreat and come at the soldiers from their sides where your bullets and arrows have a better target."

"What if there are cannons?" questioned Running Bear.

"Cannons fire only where pointed. They are slow to move and they have weaknesses. The gunpowder is in cloth bags, easy to set fire to. The canons are moved with teams of horses, shoot one of them and it takes a long time before that gun can return to fighting."

"So you say shoot fire arrows at the cannons?" said White Hawk.

"Fire at the cannons if they are on grass that will burn and at the wagons that carry the gun powder. And if possible, shoot arrows at the horses that pull them while it is dark and they are trying to get to your village."

"Why night?" questioned Running Bear.

"In the dark, a rifle makes a flame that tells where the shooter is; an arrow does not," said White Hawk, "and you knew that many battles ago."

Rusty talked for two more hours answering questions about the wise use of scouts, surprise attacks, and how organized braves fight better. He reminded them of how the Indian use of an ambush was a good example of defensive fighting. White Hawk said that was all for this day and asked if there was more in the book.

"There is more in the book, but much is about the movement of armies and things that are of little use to the Cheyenne," said Rusty. "I would still be pleased to speak with you more about this book."

"With this gift to complete the major soldier's uniform you have, we thank you for today." He gave Rusty a .44 Colt revolver.

160

"Thank you, that gift was not needed. Is this not one of the pistols from the miners that were at the fort in the stream, the last two that we chased and my father shot the last one?"

"Yes, it is like the one Tall Elk has; this was given to a brave and then traded for. Rusty...Dreams A Lot, this is a gift from the elders and no return gift is to be," said White Hawk. "I want to tell you a thing. Your uncle, Twisted Nose, likes to tell the story that when you were a lost white boy, I put my knife to you and you were this close to my cutting." He held his thumb and index finger apart by about a half an inch. There was a loose page in the book that he put between his thumb and finger, and then pulled it out, showing by the light a tiny gap. "You were really this close!" Then White Hawk laughed.

* * * * * *

Rusty sent word to Burned Face asking him to tell his friends that he would read three stories to them that night. They met in the new lodge of Running Antelope and Winter Rose. Rusty liked to change classic stories, sometimes mixing them. The ten young braves and Winter Rose, who was there as she fed them snacks of venison jerky, sat up when Rusty began with... "Once-upon-a-time there was an Indian boy, a Navaho, who watched the sheep. This tribe had sheep for their hair to make blankets with. This boy was named Pinocchio. When he was a bad boy, the medicine man put a spell on him. When Pinocchio told a lie, his nose would grow longer. One day he was bored. It was hot and not even the flies were around. He remembered the excitement when one day his brother had seen a wolf and all the braves came to chase it away. So he cried 'Wolf! A Wolf!' And braves came and he was the one they came to asking where is the wolf? 'The wolf ran away,' he lied. And his nose grew a bit longer, but only a girl saw it and no one would listen to her. The next moon, Pinocchio was again bored and cried 'Wolf! Wolf!' and all the braves came asking him where. This time he giggled and they knew he was lying. Also, the girl pointed to his nose. It was now longer. A few days later, a real wolf smelled the sheep and saw that only a little boy with a long nose was there, and he ran and took a sheep and ran to the shade to eat it. Pinocchio yelled, 'Wolf! Wolf' and no one came. The wolf saw that no braves were coming. The little girl asked a brave, 'Why don't you go? There is a wolf.' And the brave said, 'No, that is just Pinocchio, the boy that cries wolf.' The wolf saw that no one was coming and ate Pinocchio, all but his nose because it was magic. And here it is!" Rusty took from his belt a white piece of wood carved like a four-inch nose, with red paint for blood on its end and threw it at Winter Rose as he said, "And here it is!" She jumped and all the boys clapped and called for more.

For his next story, Rusty told a shortened version of *Moby Dick*. He was disappointed that it did not go over as the *Boy That Cried Wolf* had. They did not believe a fish or a canoe could be that big. He ended it and began his next.

"This story is called *The Twenty-Third Bear*. Once-upon-a-time, there was a young and powerful brave, a Cheyenne. He was tall and strong. His family had trained him to be a great hunter. He was the best at throwing a spear. One day he was asked to go after a bear that was scaring the squaws at their berry picking. He went to the Medicine Man and asked him for help. 'Wise Medicine Man, help me, I am fearful of this bear.' And the Medicine Man, who knew this was a good strong brave who could kill a bear, took the brave's spear and blew smoke on it and gave it back to the brave saying, 'Now this is a magic spear. With it you will always kill any bear as long as you are a true Cheyenne.' And the brave went and killed the bear. Then for many years, he killed bears with his spear, a spear he watched and guarded. Years later he had killed twenty and two bears, and was about to go after a giant of a grizzly bear, when he saw the same, now very old Medicine Man. He told him he was going to kill this twenty-third bear, all thanks to his magic. The man said, "Young brave, it is you, not my magic that has killed twenty and two bears. I am old and must not die with this falsehood on my lips. There is no magic on your spear. Fear not that bear. You are a great hunter and bear killer, or how else could you have killed twenty and two bears. Go and kill this bear and be proud that you did so without magic." So the brave went to kill his twenty-third bear and the bear killed and ate him. The end. There are your three stories. In a few nights I will have three more. Next buffalo hunt, please don't ask me how many buffalo I will kill. My voice is tired. Good night. He left hearing much discussion about his last story.

* * * * * *

Tall Elk came back dusty and hungry. "I go to speak to Chief Walks Fast. I will tell him that this is not a time to split the village into two halves. The same soldiers that came here with wagons and chains to trick our chiefs were at the peaceful Mandan village. They had Crow scouts that prevented the watchers from warning the few Mandan braves that were warriors. The Mandan woke to see a line of blue coat soldiers with rifles and four cannons looking at them. The soldiers said there would be no shooting if the Mandan gave up all their rifles. They fired one cannon as a warning. When the Mandan gave up their rifles, the soldiers came and searched all lodges. They took some bows and arrows, they took all spears and lances, and some tomahawks. They also took some of the better bead-worked garments and food. I will suggest to Walks Fast that we trade a few rifles and powder to the Mandan for a pony or two. The Mandan are weak, but when I was a boy, they were a powerful tribe and joined the Cheyenne in some battles."

"My arm is getting strong. I would go and shoot some buffalo for the Mandan people. I know other young braves that would go with me."

"No, but if you can ride, tell Red Falcon he may need you. We will double the watchers. Some will be far from the village, and some will watch the wagon trails. The Mandan say the soldiers came up the trail and their dust made the Mandan think it was just more wagons going west.

Rusty had to postpone his story telling to the young braves as so many were riding and watching the land around the village for miles. There was one day of excitement when Burned Face saw a Crow in a soldier's hat and chased him away.

"He did not come to fight, only to spy," was agreed to by the chiefs.

Braves are looking for a new place for the village. It is early, but Walks Fast wants a special kind of place. A place where soldiers would not have any advantage if they come.

Rusty was teased by some braves about his promise to read three more stories.

"Is your head so full of wisdom about wars and fighting that there is no room for more stories?" said Gray Wolf. Rusty knew there was some jealousy of his reading from the West Point Manual to the war chiefs.

"I will read tonight. If not all can be there, I will read a second time or they may join me when I tell stories to the Squaws."

Around an outdoor fire, Rusty held his book and spoke as if reading.

"Once upon a time, there were three young squaws. They were sisters, but two were foolish and one was wise. The two foolish ones were playing a game. The wise one was chipping flint to make a spear point. The wise sister told the foolish sisters that with the braves gone for many days, they should each make a good spear for protection. 'No,' said the first, 'I have a tomahawk, and spear-making hurts my hand.' 'No,' said the second sister, 'I have a bow and a good arrow.' The foolish two went to pick berries. When they had many berries, a bear came. He saw there were no braves near and he ran at the first sister. She threw her tomahawk. It missed and she ran home. The bear ate her basket of berries. She ran to her sister. When the bear had eaten all the first basket of berries, he came after the second foolish sister. She shot her arrow at the bear and hit the bear. It only made him mad. She dropped her basket of berries and ran with her foolish sister to their wise sister. 'Help us,' they cried, 'a bear has eaten our berries and is coming!' The wise sister told them they should have listened to her and made good strong spears like this one. When the bear came, he saw there was one more basket of berries, so he ran at the wise sister. She made as if to throw the spear. This got the bear to stop and stand on his back legs to swat the spear away, but the wise sister had not thrown the spear. She was waiting for the bear to stand. She ran and stuck him in the heart with her good spear. 'Thank you,' cried her two sisters, 'now we have bear meat.' 'No, I have bear meat. You would not listen and so I will give you some bear meat, but you must skin the bear and pick me two baskets of berries to get it.' The end." By the time Rusty had finished his story, there was such a crowd that he had to start over and tell it again.

"You still owe us two stories," said a young brave. "Tell again the story about the twenty-third bear," cried another, whose request was followed with more calls for that story.

"Very well, but that will have to be the second of tonight's three," said Rusty. He retold the story of the twenty-third bear, and stopped for a drink of water.

He told the story of Robin Hood and he changed it to Indians and bad soldiers. They enjoyed the part about the archery contest and the splitting of the winning arrow. Some braves questioned if that could be done, and made plans to test it the next day. Rusty learned later that many arrows were shot, but none split an arrow.

"Now you have to read to the young squaws," said Setting Sun.

"Later," replied Rusty. "Did you know Sam Hiller and his son, Adam, are back?"

Three days later, at first meal, Tall Elk told that the village would move in two days. For this move, Rusty was told he would be helping to herd the ponies.

"A brave has found good place, and for this move, many braves will ride far around the tribe to prevent any spies from seeing the move. After we have moved many miles, and when the wind is from the west, a grass fire will be made to cover the move."

"Then the Cheyenne are running and hiding?" asked Setting Sun.

"That is right and wise," said an irritated Tall Elk who got up and left.

"I am sorry," said Setting Sun, "that was a foolish thing for me to say. I'll go tell Father so."

"Setting Sun has something on her head. She is like a girl with a problem she can't talk about," said Cloud Woman.

"She has been speaking with Sam Hiller and his son, Adam," said Rusty.

"I have news for you," said Cloud Woman. "That mask you had made for Eyes Down is good. She now wears it all day while beading clothes. We made her try it just inside our beading lodge for a short time, then half a day. She now says it is good. She sees more look at her when speaking to her with the mask on. We are after her to wear it around the village. She is still afraid people will laugh. That girl speaks a lot of your storytelling. Tell, read, tonight, and I will come and bring her and her mask."

"And I shall have Setting Sun speak to her friends, and they will behave nice to that unfortunate girl. I will see to that," said Walking Dove.

Rusty's reading to the braves outside of a lodge was so successful that he decided to do the same for the young squaws. He made a trade with two ten-year-old boys to keep his fire going for lessons with throwing his javelin. He had been told not to charge for lessons with the sling; nothing was said about the javelin, he decided. On the edge of the village at a place where pine trees blocked the constant high prairie wind, he moved a tree stump to sit on as he told his stories. There were more girls than ever. Before at this storytelling he saw some he did not know. Cloud Woman and Walking Dove escorted Eyes Down to a darker corner. She looked lovely. Her dress had once belonged to Setting Sun, but had been remade by Cloud Woman. Walking Dove made sure Rusty saw her.

"We want to hear *Romeo and Juliet* again," cried many girls. Setting Sun said her friends wanted to hear the story about the twenty-third bear that the braves were arguing about.

"Once-upon-a-time," Rusty began, then he stopped to say he would honor the requests, but first would read a new story. He heard Setting Sun snicker. She knew his stories were not coming from the book he was holding.

"Long before the Indians knew the horse and rifle, the Arapaho used a pit to kill buffalo. A deep hole, a pit with steep sides, was made. It would be covered with a few strong tree limbs and then straw and dirt and grass until it could not be seen. A brave would wave a red cloth at a buffalo bull and get him so mad he would chase the brave. The brave would know where to put his feet on the limbs and run over the pit. The buffalo would fall into it and could be killed with lances. The limbs would be used to climb in and to carry out the hide, meat and bones. Then the Indians got horses, then guns, and the pit was not used, but it was there. The Apache won that land from the Arapaho and the pit. A very brave young Arapaho squaw named Pony Girl was coming down from a high mountain with fine flint rocks to make arrowheads, when she was caught in a snowstorm so heavy she could not see. She was sure she would die and prayed to her spirits for help. Then she found a cave. This cave smelled of mountain lion. She had no choice but to stay. She used her flint and some dry grass that the wind spirits had put in the cave and made a fire. Then she saw it...a big mountain lion. But this lion was sick. His ribs showed. He had not eaten for days, his front paws were stuck with porcupine needles. To him, the girl was food. He tried to crawl at her on his side because he could not stand. All he would be able to do was bite her. His claws were full of needles. The girl felt pity for him. She began to pull out the needles. He saw that she was helping him and made no more move to bite her. When the last needle was out, she made her fire bigger, to protect her, but the big lion left. The snowstorm was still filling the air with heavy snow. When the lion came back, he had a mountain sheep. He bit off a leg and pushed it to the girl. When the snow stopped, she left.

"One day, five years later, Pony Girl was taken by the raiding Apache. She was given to an evil brave with an ugly nose and bad smelling teeth. She ran away and was caught. She ran away again and was caught. Beatings would not make her stay with this brave. One night a mountain lion fell into the buffalo pit and was trapped. 'Don't shoot arrows into the lion. I have a use for him.' The brave with the bad teeth dragged Pony Girl to the pit and told her he would throw her to that lion unless she said she would no more run away. 'I would rather the lion eat me than sleep with you,' she said. So he threw her into the pit to the snarling mountain lion. The lion was about to bite her when he smelled her and knew this was the girl that pulled the porcupine needles from his paws. The Apache could not believe the lion was not biting the girl. 'Wait until dark. He will be hungry by then and eat her.' Pony Girl climbed on the back of the lion and he jumped out of the pit with her. She rode him until she met some Arapaho braves. The end. That is story number one." Until there was cheering and clapping, Rusty was not sure they liked the story, they were so quiet.

"Do you really want to hear the story about the bear?"

"Yes! We do," said Setting Sun and her friends. He told the same story he had told the braves as best he could remember. He again ended it with the bear killing the brave who no longer believed his spear was magic.

"Is that all it is about!" exclaimed Setting Sun. "Any fool can see he lost his nerve. And some boys said we would not get the ending! They must think the heads of squaws are hollow and only for growing hair?"

"Do *Romeo and Juliet*!"

Rusty had been told he should count on this being requested. He made a knife of deerskin painted silver and made stiff with tallow. As before, he reversed the deaths by poison and dagger so he, playing Romeo, could stab himself. He over-acted with it and at the ending, stabbed himself with a great swing of the blade at his chest, and fell, rolling over and playing dead. The effect was better than he hoped for. A young squaw screamed, "He's dead! He killed himself just to entertain us!" Rusty had to bite his tongue to keep playing dead. Soon Setting Sun had enough and pulled him up. Then he bowed and said that was all for tonight. He was partway back to his lodge when the girl, Cricket, stopped him. "You must let me pull on your string later tonight when my older brother sleeps. Please say yes." He said, "Yes." The broken arm had healed at last. It had taken almost three months.

When it was dark and the lodge fire was out, Rusty felt a tug on the string tied to his foot. Under his sleeping shirt he was dressed. He quietly went out to find not Cricket, but Red Cloud. A girl as beautiful as any he had seen. "I am new to the village of Walks Fast, but have heard of the storyteller Dream A Lot. Let us go to the stream where we can wash after."

At what should have been the most private part of the stream, he saw a white doeskin dress on the grass, then Setting Sun standing in the water with a man. They walked farther downstream. He was sure Setting Sun had not seen him.

Back at the lodge, he rolled back into his sleeping robe and did not tie on the string. *Cricket will have to wait for another night,* he thought. When he was breathing like he was sleeping, Setting Sun returned. She saw the string rolled up by his side and tied it to his foot and put the end out of the lodge and went to her bed. In the middle of the night, Rusty woke to find his foot pulled by the string. He was half awake. *Well,* he thought, *I did tell her she could come.* He went out and she hugged him. It was not Cricket, it was Eyes Down.

"Rusty, let me show you how grateful I am for your helping me." She led him to the pine trees where she had placed a blanket. When he saw her undressed, his urge was far greater than his fatigue. The first time was painful—he learned it was her first.

"I have been told the second time is better," she said holding him so tight he could not leave even if he had the strength or willpower; he had neither.

Rusty was just in the door flap when he fell asleep. Setting Sun was not. She tied the string to his foot, while just able to suppress laughing out loud. In the darkness of late night, Cricket pulled and pulled on the string. It had been very hard for her to get away. She had bragged to an older girl about her sleeping with Rusty. Pulling on the string did not bring him out. She reached in and pulled Rusty to the door flap. He looked at her and said, "Not tonight." But she would not leave. At last she got him to go with her. On the banks of the stream she wanted him to swim with her to wake him up. While she undressed to swim, he fell back to sleeping. That was too much of an insult for her. She left him there.

Setting Sun became worried. She found Rusty sleeping by the stream. It would be light soon. Tall Elk would be mad.

She woke Walking Dove and the two of them carried him and put him back in the lodge. Walking Dove took the string.

At first meal, all ate but Rusty.

"Let him sleep," said Walking Dove.

When he did wake and asked to eat, only Cloud Woman was there. As he ate, she held up the string. "This fire needs more to burn," she said as she let him see her put the string in the cooking fire. Rusty nodded his head and with a feeble voice said, "Yes."

Chapter 15

Rusty rode all around the new village site. He was proud, but could tell no one. He was sure his speaking about war with White Hawk played a part in the selection of this place. What looked at first as one small village was, in fact, three villages, all close but hidden by trees. The only approach from the high prairie led to an opening in the trees not fifty feet wide. It was a place that did look down on the lodges. There was a place for a small pony herd nearby. Only by riding down narrow trails could you get to the other villages. There were many trees on both sides of the clearing above the village, and the low brushes had not been burned for years.

Rusty was having first meal when Setting Sun whispered to him, "I want to speak with you in private. Meet me where the stream has the little waterfalls." Then she left. Before he could go, Tall Elk asked him if he would like to go and help. "I have found some Sioux braves that I might trade the horse Samson to."

"Now?"

"No, there is no hurry, they are trading with other braves, but before the sun is high."

Setting Sun led Rusty to a place on the stream.

"Don't you just love this place? Look at the color of the trees and the sun making the little waterfalls sparkle."

"Is that what you have me here for?" asked Rusty.

She took his hand and faced him. "Brother that I do love, I am going to leave someday soon. I have learned a way by speaking with Sam Hiller, the gun buyer friend of the Cheyenne. I will slip away, and only my mother will know, and you. You can please help keep Tall Elk from sending braves to stop me."

"Where are you going? Not all the way to Quebec for your Hudson Bay money!"

"No, not all the way. The one-hundred English pounds that is to be mine, left to me by my real father, is money I can use to go to this Ireland place and see my uncle and the land my father spoke of so many times when I was a little girl. I plan to come back. There is a something you could give me to take."

"What?"

"I would like to have one of the dueling pistols to carry."

"Yes, but you have the six-shot Colt."

"I will take the Colt. It is heavy and only when I carry a large bag will I have it. Cloud Woman made a way for you to have the dueling pistol hidden on your person."

"Yes, how soon? Which way will you go?"

"I will leave when I can. How soon, I can't say, as I don't know. Don't worry, I have a plan. I will have some braves go part way. South of here on the Platte there now are riverboats that go all the way to the Missouri River, and steam paddleboats from there to the city, St. Louis. There will be a bank where I can ask for help. The Hudson Bay people have a bank or place to do their trading in New York. There is also where I get to ride a big ship to this Ireland. I have words on my letter from my uncle in Dublin. Don't worry, I will be safe. I also have the long knife you made for me. So if I leave and don't see...a boy with white hair that blushed to red...goodbye." Then she hugged him and ran off.

* * * * * *

"You are taking this many ponies to trade?" asked Rusty as he rode with Tall Elk.

"No, they are part of the way you look when you trade, like you have many and don't have to trade. See, I ride Samson. I will speak of trading that one, and let the Sioux talk me into trading the horse I ride."

Rusty could not wait till the trading was over...it took so long. He was thinking about making up a funny story about horse trading when Tall Elk called to him.

"Go tell your mother I am going to the Sioux village. I will be back in two or three days. If you will come, bring food and be here soon." Rusty did as told, and the next day at the Sioux village he learned there was more than horse trading to this visit. Tall Elk did trade the horse Samson, but for only three, including one that had won many races.

The war chief of the Sioux spoke to Rusty. He was feeling proud he had been allowed to smoke a pipe and sit with these chiefs. Rusty heard his father speak about the white soldiers and what they had done to the Mandan.

"I hear you have great wisdom and can know what some men say before they speak. Thank you for coming here," was said to Rusty. The Sioux chief, Lone Bear, then spoke to Tall Elk. "Will Tall Elk have his son, Dream A Lot, share with their Sioux friends the words this son says the white soldiers put in a book on how they make war? If that is true."

"It is true. They have books that they use to teach the officers, the white war chiefs, how to make war. Shall I tell you one of their ways? And shall I tell the Sioux what I told White Hawk on how to defeat them?" There were nods to go on. Rusty reviewed most of what he had said about offense and defense and the use of cannons and their weaknesses. He could tell Tall Elk was pleased. When the fire was allowed to die down, they were guided to lodges to spend the night. Rusty was taken to a lodge that was empty. He had expected to be fed, and maybe given a gift for his words. He was sitting on a rolled up buffalo hide when a very lovely young squaw came in holding a blanket around herself. He took a deep breath. *Could this be his gift?* he wondered. Then she opened the blanket and he saw that she was holding a steaming pot of food. There were bowls and horn spoons on a piece of tree bark that she pointed to. "What is your name?" he asked speaking in Sioux.

She was surprised he spoke Sioux.

"I am called Fast Bee Catcher. When you have had food, would the great storyteller share one small story with me and my friends?"

Soon there were five girls and an older squaw that had to be there to keep an eye on him. He told the story of the girl and the lion, then a short version of *Romeo and Juliet*. When he was done and the older squaw made it plain the girls were to leave, he stopped them from clapping, saying that the polite way to give thanks to a storyteller was with hugs and kisses. He wondered himself if he was joking or going way too far. The older squaw spoke in words he knew that this was not so. He was lying. The girl, Fast Bee Catcher, left, getting his eyes and making a strange movement with her hand on her leg. He didn't know that sign. *I have got to have a girl teach me what these signs they make mean*, he thought.

They got back to the lodge at a time to eat. Walking Dove looked at them and Rusty saw her eyes were red. The same for Cloud Woman. Tall Elk looked around the lodge and saw that things of Setting Sun were missing.

"Our daughter, Late Setting Sun, she makes up her head that she is a woman and can do as she pleases. She is gone!" said Walking Dove who could say no more because of crying.

"When? How? Shall I go after her? Who is the brave?" questioned Tall Elk.

"No brave, as you think. She has left saying she will be back some year." Walking Dove had to stop due to her crying.

Cloud Woman spoke, her voice weak. "Setting Sun is going to the land of Quinn. Adam, son of Sam Hiller, is helping her part of the way. He knows how the white people travel. Don't send after her. I believe she will be back. I hope I live that long." Then she began to cry and that got Walking Dove to cry also.

"Did you know of this?"

"Only that it was to happen some time. She never told me when. It looks like she picked a time when you would be gone. My sister is well armed. She asked me one day for the use of one of my dueling pistols from Cry A Lot boy's uncle. And she has the six-shot Colt pistol and the knife I made her. I should feel sorry for the man that tried to do her wrong. Excuse me, I am tearful speaking about her and she is not gone long." He saw a strange look on Tall Elk, as if a man does not have tears. So he joked. "I must go. It will take some time to find a girl to tease me like my sister."

* * * * * *

Two Cheyenne braves with the new Golden Boy Henry rifles rode to the river with Setting Sun and Adam. They had been traveling sixteen days. Lone Pony had spoken to Adam and learned there was no love between Adam and Setting Sun, but she had slept with him as a way to get his help. He would take her as far as St. Louis. There was a small cabin and a dock, but no boat was near. Adam called and learned the boat south would be there in two days.

"Shall we stay and wait with you?" questioned Lone Pony.

"No, we shall be safe. Come here." Setting Sun gave each brave a hug, kiss and, to their surprise, a small bit of her hair that she cut off.

"I won't want these, put them on your lance for luck."
Lone Pony and the other brave rode off, but soon Lone Pony
returned with a small deer. "Here, have good meat. This is
all you will need for two days. If I did not shoot it, you
would shoot three buffalo again," he said teasing her.

* * * * * *

Two days later, Tall Elk came into the lodge with a
white man's shovel.

"My friend, Sam Hiller, tells that white soldiers fighting
in the war back east dig into the earth to hide from bullets
like prairie dogs. I believe he is right. You say that staying in
the lodge is how you fight, then dig a hole. The soldiers will
be here in the morning."

Scouts had spotted the blue coat soldiers moving toward
the village the day before. This time, Crow scouts were only
allowed to see what Walks Fast wanted them to see. What
looked like Cheyenne hunting parties blocked their finding
the whole village. Cloud Woman and Walking Dove refused
to leave their lodge. So did a few others. But most of the
tribe listened carefully to what the war chiefs said. Sam
Hiller was still there. He spoke to Rusty.

"Boy, listen to me. I am not taking part in this fight no
matter how much the Cheyenne mean to me. I am a white
man. To the whites I am a renegade, an outlaw of the worst
kind, a traitor to be hung with a trial. You are walking down
the same trail."

"Stop, these are my people. I was adopted by Tall Elk. I
can't leave, and I can help them win."

"Rusty, suit yourself. I ride north. Keep your head
down. Wait, if you are going to get into this fight, use your
head. Forget about the trying to fool the army with the
major's uniform. One look at your face and they would lock
you up for a hanging. No major I ever met had freckles, not
even the few you still have. Consider being a sniper. Good
luck." He left. Rusty saw him stop and talk to Twisted Nose.

"Rusty, my nephew, I have spoke to Sam Hiller and Tall Elk. The soldiers will be here soon. Find a tree and take your Hawkins rifle and a rope. Your duty will be to stay where you can watch the lodges on this end. Shoot only those soldiers that would set fire to the village. You should only need your rifles; let a trusted friend use your Colt pistol. Choose your tree carefully," said Twisted Nose.

Rusty gave his Colt pistol to Burned Face. "Just to use for this fight."

He returned to the lodge and changed into his white man's clothing. When Walking Dove asked why, he said, "These are dark and I will be hard to see, that is all, and the pockets will hold my spare bullets better than a bag."

Rusty found a pine tree where he would be fifty yards from the lodges and just under two hundred from the clearing overlooking the village where it was believed the soldiers would take a firing position. With rope, he hung the Colt rifle over his shoulder. He climbed with one arm holding his Hawkins rifle. *The last thing I can let happen is to fall and break an arm,* he thought. He soon wished he had not climbed the tree so early. Nothing was happening.

From his high perch he saw Crow and blue coat cavalry run off the small horse herd. The few boys guarding it ran calling that soldiers were coming. Rusty saw many braves hide from the stream bank, not forty yards from the village and less than one hundred yards from the clearing. The cavalry rose up fast. Many were the black soldiers the Indians called buffalo soldiers. They had the newest uniforms. They dismounted and one man in four took horses to the rear. It was the Fourth Cavalry, and was two companies, but they were far short of the two hundred men called for. The total was about one hundred and eighty. Of those, one in four was not in action, holding horses. Twenty manned the four cannons and a few others stood around in charge or waiting to run messages. The officer lined them up in two rows facing the village. The four cannons were pulled by horses to a place behind them and set to fire over their heads. While they assembled, twenty or so Cheyenne walked around the village manning cooking fires and acting as if the soldiers were only so many blue trees.

When the captain in charge said it was time, a young lieutenant stepped forward. He had what looked like a rolled up fat tube of wood he used to make his voice louder. He called for the chiefs to come and speak. There was no response. The captain blew, and one cannon fired a shot that went over the stream. With that, many unseen braves began to move close to the ends of the row of soldiers.

The lieutenant called that they came in peace. No one paid any attention to him, yet he continued.

"People of the Cheyenne, to keep peace, your Great White Father requires that you turn in all your rifles. The White Father will send you cattle and blankets. You have three minutes to begin putting down all guns or the cannon will fire."

Rusty desperately wanted to shoot him as a liar. The captain raised his sword, but before he could bring it down, he turned his head. The officer in charge of the cannon was yelling. Fire arrows were falling on the wagon with the cannon powder. The horses waiting to move the cannons were being shot. Smoke was starting to drift towards them from a grass fire behind them. The captain dropped his sword and called for his men to fire. They fired, but mostly at empty lodges. The braves at the stream took aim and fired many rifles, resting their guns on the edge of the stream bank and giving the soldiers only small targets. Many of the troopers of Fourth Cavalry dropped dead or were wounded. The captain now had an enemy he could see and called for a charge.

Out of the woods on both sides, two hundred screaming Cheyenne braves ran at them. Rusty looked for someone to shoot. Every time he took aim, that man fell before he could shoot. He fired at one that was trying to get a cannon working in spite of a grass fire that had scared off the gun crew. Rusty shot him but saw his target fall with a leg wound. Something shiny caught Rusty's attention. It was an officer on a horse in the rear. He was holding a brass telescope and looking at the smoke from Rusty's rifle. He was well over two hundred yards. Rusty took aim, but the man put spurs on his horse and ran. Rusty tried to yell and point to the man, but the noise was too great. Only a few of the soldiers that charged made it to the village. Braves and squaws were coming out of lodges and shooting them, many from behind them. Rusty saw a buffalo soldier fly off his feet. The smoke cleared and Rusty saw Cloud Woman standing and reloading her shotgun. Five soldiers, their rifles empty, gave up, dropped their guns and raised their hands. They were in the middle of the village. Braves and squaws moved around them. None shot or went after them until one man pulled a pistol from under his shirt, and shot one of the Fat Bellies, then put the gun to his head and fired. With that, all were killed. Rusty looked around. Behind him away from the fighting he saw a blue coat crawling in the brush. It was a black man, one of the buffalo soldiers. A boy also saw the soldier and went at him with a tiny bow and arrow. When he pointed his pistol at the boy, Rusty shot him with the Colt rifle. He shot him a second time to be sure. Then he began to climb down.

He could see the fighting on the ridge was over, only wounded soldiers were left. He went to the man he had shot and picked up the pistol. It was a revolver, but not a Colt. On the barrel it said Remington. He liked the way it felt better than the Colt, so he rolled the man over and took off his belt and pistol holster. As an after thought, he checked the man's pockets and found a wad of paper money and a few coins. He asked a young brave to hold his two rifles and ran up to the many dead cavalry. He started pulling money from pockets, and some squaws saw him. They were taking rings and coins and things like knives, and all the tobacco.

"Here," one called, "give the paper to Rusty, he will know what it is for."

When he got back to get his rifles, his pockets were bulging with greenbacks.

"Did you count coups?" asked Tall Elk.

Rusty took him to the one he had shot. "I am now a renegade to the whites. And I was seen by a white soldier. Did any catch the one that ran away on a gray horse?"

"I will ask. I don't know of any that got away. Walks Fast will want you to tell him of that."

It was such a victory that the torturing of the few wounded was quick. At the fire, Walks Fast spoke first.

"This captain did not lie. He said a Great White Father would give the Cheyenne what we need. He came to take our rifles, but gave us many more. I will have Dream A Lot...Rusty send him a letter of thanks!"

* * * * * *

"You are sure? I could trade a pony." said a surprised Burned Face.

"No, my friend, keep the pistol, it was a gift I got just for words. I have this pistol I like better, and I earned it." He showed the Remington. The praise heaped on Rusty for the words he gave to the war chiefs from the West Point book did not make his mood improve.

I am a renegade, a white not welcome by whites, yet is this the life I want for all time? he thought.

He learned the next day the village would move soon. The many dead cavalry would be left to the wolves. Sam Hiller came back and suggested that the cannon be hidden. The cannon was pulled to a bed of quicksand and pushed under. Sam Hiller being there did not help Rusty's mood. And without Setting Sun, the lodge was not the same. Rusty was picking up things to move and found the calendar. In one week he would be sixteen. He took a long walk. A girl asked when he would read a story and was shocked when he said, "Maybe never."

After his walk, he found Sam Hiller and asked him to go with him to see Tall Elk and Walking Dove. "It is time for me to take a leave. I need to find out if I am to be a white man living as a Cheyenne and labeled a renegade, or a white man in the white man's world that has been trained as a Cheyenne. The only way to know is to visit my white family. No matter what path, I will come back.

"I asked Sam Hiller to be here because he was there when White Hawk and Twisted Nose found me, so this is my new beginning. Also, I welcome his advice on how I can safely go to St. Louis.

It will be some time before I return to stay or tell I am not staying. Maybe I will go and find my sister, Late Setting Sun and drag her back."

He feared becoming a renegade white man hated by his own race.